For Zach & Rachel...
Love you both and
appreciate your support. ♡

jclafler

A LEAP

of

FAITH

A LEAP

~of~

FAITH

J.C. LAFLER

REDEMPTION
PRESS

Published by Redemption Press, PO Box 427, Enumclaw, WA 98022

Toll Free (844) 2REDEEM (273-3336)

Redemption Press is honored to present this title in partnership with the author. The views expressed or implied in this work are those of the author. Redemption Press provides our imprint seal representing design excellence, creative content, and high quality production.

ISBN: 978-1-68314-660-5
    978-1-68314-661-2 (hardcover)
    978-1-68314-662-9 (ePub)
    978-1-68314-663-6 (Mobi)

Library of Congress Catalog Card Number: 2018947698

He reached down from heaven and rescued me;
he drew me out of deep waters.
Psalm 18:16 (NLT)

Acknowledgments

I would like to dedicate this story to a young lady and her mother whom I have known for many years, Courtney and Sharon Johnson. They have been good friends for a long time, and Sharon encouraged me to publish my first book before it was even completed. She holds a special place in my heart, and I have watched her daughter, Courtney, grow into a beautiful, caring young woman with a voice like an angel. I couldn't resist putting a bit of them and their names in this story. Thank you so much for your love and support over the years. It means the world to me.

I would also like to offer a huge *thank-you* to Athena Dean Holtz and the wonderful team of professionals at Redemption Press. You have become my friends as well as my publisher, and I am so happy to be one of your authors. God bless all of you, and thank you for working with me, praying for me, and making this whole process about God first!

Chapter 1

Atlantic Beach, Florida

When Hurricane Ester crashed onto the shores of Courtney's hometown, everyone in its path feared nothing would ever be the same again. An unusually warm November had lulled them all into thinking the hurricane season was past. The weather forecast on the morning news indicated the storm forming off the coast would not make shore. But by afternoon, things were different. The storm was turning unexpectedly and heading right in their direction!

Terrified of the coming storm, sixteen-year-old Courtney Alexander had already made one trip outside, begging her mom and stepfather to come in. "The storm is turning toward us. Come in the house, please!" she begged her mom again.

"We have plenty of time," her stepfather called back from the pier next to their dock. He kept his left arm tightly around her mom as the wind whipped at their hair and peppered their clothing with salty spray. Clinging to the railing with the other hand, he refused to heed Courtney's warnings, although she could see them struggling to hold on to the railing.

She raced down the dock, wanting only to get back inside. She thought she heard her mom calling, "Courtney!" Glancing back, she watched in horror as they were swept off the pier.

"Mom!" Her scream blew back into her throat, with a wind strong enough to bend the backyard palms to the ground. She barely made it back to their yard before the swirling wind and water headed in her direction. Changing her mind in a split second, she turned and snatched up a heavy piece of rope hanging over the post at the end of the dock. She ran for the park up the hill from the beach. Once there she knotted the rope around her body and ran for the big steel post that supported the tower, overlooking the park. Running around and around the post until she had used up all the rope, she managed to secure herself to the post.

She would never forget the shock of the wind and water tearing at her. Surely she would drown or get swept away, post and all. She tried to scream, hoping someone would hear her and come to her rescue, but the wind whipped her voice away.

"God . . . help . . . me!" Her voice came out in gasps. "I'm sorry! I know I turned my back on you when Daddy died, but I need you to help me be strong and make the wind and rain stop. Please!" She knew only He could provide the miracle she needed. Without it, her life could be over. As she slumped down within the rope wrapped around her, she thought she heard a whisper.

I am here.

It seemed like forever before the storm finally stopped. Courtney was barely conscious as the day faded into night. The storm raged on, taking her breath away over and over. When she finally realized she could breathe without struggling, she brushed the wet hair out of her eyes and looked around in amazement. Her clothes were soaked, the water up to her neck, but the rope had held her fast to the pole. The sun was rising, bringing daylight that allowed her to look in disbelief at her surroundings. While she could see broken swings and the curve of a slide floating amid other debris, the post tower had somehow remained intact. But that was about the only thing left. Destruction littered the area around her as far as she could see. And the park on the hill was barely above the water level. She felt bruised and beaten, and despite the whisper she'd heard the night before, she was all alone—no help in sight.

She unwound the heavy, wet rope and worked her way loose from the pole. Pulling herself up the metal steps to the tower above, she looked around. The entire area was flooded. Chimneys stuck up out of the water where houses had been. Some of the trees had uprooted and floated along with trash cans and windows and other items that had washed away in the storm. An empty metal boat bobbed along in the water, along with a plastic mattress, a bicycle, and a cooler. She turned in the direction of her home. Nothing remained of it. She couldn't help the twinge of relief that came as she imagined her stepfather gone forever. But she would give anything for another chance to see her mom. She fingered the locket around her neck that had belonged to her mother and her grandmother before her. Her mom had trusted her to take care of it, and for now it was all she had. The tower swayed as a strong gust of wind swept by, and Courtney realized she had to get somewhere safe.

The metal boat had snagged in a couple of broken trees near the park, and she made a hasty decision. She climbed down the steps, gathered the wet rope that had saved her life, and jumped into the water. She headed toward the trees, and by inching out along the branches, she could just grasp the boat's edge. Balancing carefully, she pulled it toward her and climbed in, taking the rope with her. Once settled in the boat, she grabbed a nearby bucket as it floated by and bailed out the water. She pulled the branches away and broke free of the tree. Then, using the oars that had miraculously stayed in the oar brackets on either side of the boat, she pushed out into the swirling waters.

Chapter 2

Within an hour the rain had all but stopped, and the wind had died down. She steered around and around the chimney of her home, looking for any sign of her mom. There was nothing. Fingering the locket again, she tried to tell herself there was still a chance her mom had survived, but couldn't stop the tears. She had to find help. As the current moved her toward what she believed was the closest town, Courtney began to grab items she thought she could use as they floated by: a plastic jug, an old tool bag, a small cooler, and a blanket in a zipped plastic bag. She tucked them all under the boat's seat. As the sun came out and the wind dried her clothes, she started singing the last song she had been listening to on the radio before the storm broke. Her voice echoed across the water, and she actually felt better for a moment, until her tears began to fall again, and her song turned into sobs.

Then something caught her eye——an infant seat coming toward the boat with a bright orange life jacket strapped around it! Without thinking she secured her oars and snatched the seat, life jacket and all, as it came along the side of the boat. Struggling with its weight, she lifted it into the boat. As she sat it upright in the bottom of the boat, and pulled away a wet blanket strapped in the seat, a pair of bright-blue eyes gazed at her—a tiny baby still strapped in the seat! As they gazed at each other, she realized that someone had lost their baby.

As the boat sailed along, Courtney brought her attention back to keeping the boat afloat in the sometimes-churning flood waters. She needed to find a place to stop and check the baby out more thoroughly, but for now she steered the boat in the direction she thought would lead her to the next town, where she might get help. Sirens blared in the far distance. If she could just make it to their location before nightfall . . . She figured it was still late morning, since she had seen the sun rise.

The water was calmer now, and the baby was starting to doze, despite being damp. Courtney hooked the oars into their brackets and took a second to check the baby. Someone had placed the child into a plastic bag up to her shoulders and had tucked a bottle and diapers down in the bottom of the bag, then had wrapped the blanket tightly around her. Everything was pink, including the blanket, so she was pretty sure the baby was a girl. The bag had protected her clothing, which was only damp. The baby seat must have stayed upright as it sailed through the water like a miniature boat, the life jacket keeping it up out of most of the water.

Now the sun was starting to dry her out and warm her. Courtney picked up the blanket, spread it over the seat to dry, and picked up the oars. She sang softly as they floated along in calmer waters. She smiled a little as the infant drifted off to sleep, suddenly having much more than herself to think about.

By the time the sun was high in the sky, Courtney was starting to tire. She thought she saw land in the distance, but she couldn't be sure. Her arms ached from trying to steer the boat. The boat was full of the items she had tried to salvage, and she felt like she was sitting in the middle of a flea market. The baby was awake, after sleeping for what seemed like hours to Courtney. Her cheeks were very rosy, so Courtney had draped the blanket between the two seats on the boat to provide shade and protection for the baby. The blanket was dry now, but she left it in place over the baby's seat.

She saw the top of a building up ahead, with a cross sticking up on its roof. She recognized it as a church she had admired many times when traveling to a nearby town for shopping. As she floated closer, she noticed the stained-glass windows had all been blown out and only the top floor remained above water. Suddenly, she realized that she was going to run right into the building. The water swirling around the church as it settled was sucking her in! Trying to steer to one side, her tired arms resisted. Before she could maneuver any farther, she struck the building head-on with a thump, running the front end of the boat right into one of the large open windows. "No!" Courtney said out loud. How in the world was she going to get the boat free of the window?

Chapter 3

Carefully edging her way to the front of the boat, Courtney surveyed the inside of the building. She was looking at the upper floor of the church, which had a couple of inches of standing water but otherwise seemed intact. Padded chairs and broken stained-glass window pieces littered the room. Courtney dragged her gaze back to where the boat was actually stuck in the open window, snagged tight on the broken window frame. What to do now? She would have to break the boat free of the tangled wood. Maybe the old tool bag had something she could use.

Hearing the baby starting to fuss, Courtney made her way to the middle of the boat and pushed aside the blanket. Frightened blue eyes looked back at her, and her heart melted when she saw fresh tears staining the baby's cheeks. Sitting back down, she realized for the first time in hours she didn't have to work at steering the boat and had both hands free. She unbuckled the baby and held her close. Watching apprehensively to make sure the boat was not going to jar loose with the movement, she reached under the seat for the bag that held the diapers and bottle. After changing the baby, she pulled out the bottle and noticed it had powder in the bottom. Courtney unscrewed the top of the bottle, took a sniff, and was certain it contained some kind of powdered formula. Knowing from her experience babysitting that you usually just add water, she realized that she was going to have to use one of the precious bottles of water she had rescued in her travels. Opening one, she carefully poured it into the baby's bottle, shaking it gently until all of the powder was dissolved. The water was warm from sitting in the boat, so that helped. Picking up the fussing baby, she placed the nipple of the bottle near her mouth. The baby sucked the bottle hungrily. After her feeding, the baby dozed, so Courtney placed her back in her infant seat for a nap.

Making her way back to the front of the boat that was caught in the window, Courtney surveyed her choices. She could try to free the boat and move on, or she could climb inside the church and see if it would provide rest and shelter for the night. She grabbed the rope that had saved her life and tied it securely to a large curtain hook just inside the window, looping the remainder of the rope around one of the seats inside the boat. After looking back and seeing the baby fast asleep under the protective blanket, she decided to see what was inside. Climbing gingerly onto the open ledge of the window, Courtney lowered herself inside.

The floor inside the church was uneven from being battered by the storm, and some parts of the room had quite a bit of standing water. Making her way up a couple of carpeted steps at one end of the room, she realized that this must have been the sanctuary, as there was still a large cross on the front wall of the room and a raised platform. A pit at one side of the platform was filled with water that looked much cleaner than the water outside, and Courtney remembered a similar place at the church where she had been baptized. Closing her eyes, she could still picture her father holding her hand as their pastor led her into the baptismal pool. She smiled as she remembered her excitement in repeating the words about accepting Jesus Christ as her Savior and saw the pride on her father's face once more. Oh, to be able to go back to those days, with her father at her side! She missed him so much and felt like God had deserted them when her father got ill. After he died, she couldn't bring herself to trust in God. She shook the thoughts aside, trying to focus on her current situation.

Looking around the sanctuary, Courtney thought this might be a good place to stop for the night. She could gather enough chairs to make an area to sleep and be up off the floor if the water rose. She might even be able to wash up a bit and get a little sleep. She was terrified to think about spending the night in the boat once it was dark. It would be difficult to steer around debris in the dark, and she wouldn't be able to see where they were going. Besides, she was exhausted.

Making her way back to the window, she saw the infant still asleep under the blanket and set about making them a place for the night. She quickly gathered eight of the padded chairs and made two rows of four facing each other, pushing them tight together to form an area where she could lie down. She added an additional chair at one end where she could set the baby's chair. It wasn't a bed, but it would do. At least the church platform was at the very front of the church, away from the open window, which would give them protection from the weather.

She retrieved the baby from the boat, lifting her down and inside out of the way as she jumped lightly into the church. She carried her up to the platform and sat her on the chair at the end of her makeshift bed. She returned for as much of the "stuff" she had gathered as she thought they might need, including the tool bag she hoped would provide a means for loosening the boat when morning came. Each trip took time, and by the time she had everything inside she, the sun was beginning to go down.

Courtney turned her attention to the baby. She didn't know how old the little girl was, but she was very tiny and slept often, so she would guess around six to eight weeks. She changed her diaper one more time, wrapped her back in the now-dry blanket, and tucked her back into her infant seat. The baby was asleep almost instantly. Courtney knew she would want another bottle before long, but that would be a problem for later. She was tired and sore and wanted nothing more than to climb onto the chairs and close her eyes. She splashed water from the pool on her face and arms and dried them on her shirt. She washed the blood off her left leg, where something sharp had gouged it in the storm, making sure it was clean. Then she unzipped the blanket she had found floating in the plastic bag. It was soft and dry, so she pulled it over her and tried to position herself on the lined-up chairs. As she lay there, she noticed the letters etched on a sign that was still hanging on the wall beside her: *For by grace you have been saved through faith, and that not of yourselves, it is the gift of God. Ephesians 2:8.*

Still confused about God's role in her father's illness, the verse did not provide the comfort that it should have. Still, it was her last thought as she fell fast asleep.

Chapter 4

Courtney floated weightlessly in the small pool. It felt so good to forget about everything and just float carelessly in the cool water. Suddenly she noticed her stepfather watching her through the open window, and she sank down in the water, realizing she was naked!

"Go away!" she tried to scream. She saw him trying to find a way to climb into the window. As she tried to touch the bottom of the pool in an effort to get out, she noticed the pool had gotten much deeper and the water had started to swirl around her with bits of debris everywhere. She thought she heard a baby crying. Why would there be a baby crying?

Courtney woke up with a start, knocking over one of the chairs as she sat up. She heard the baby crying clearly now and realized she had been dreaming. Shaking off the remainder of the dream, she picked up the crying infant and snuggled her close.

"Don't cry, little one," she crooned. "I will take care of you!" The baby quieted as Courtney snuggled her and sang her a little tune. Then she laid her on the chairs and picked up the bag that still held a couple of diapers. Taking one out, she unsnapped the baby's sleeper and got rid of the soiled diaper, quickly replacing it with a fresh one. She picked up the little girl and walked over to the window, noticing that the sun had started to rise.

It was odd to be standing there, looking out at a large expanse of water, feeling alone in the world except for the little infant snuggled on her shoulder. It brought out protective instincts that she didn't even know she possessed.

Everything looked surreal in the early morning light, and yesterday's problems had all but disappeared. Courtney's only concern at the moment was to survive long enough to get somewhere safe where help was available. She couldn't hear sirens this morning, but she still thought she could see land in the far distance. If only she could get this boat back in the water and make her way in that direction . . .

Her stomach growled, but there was no food available. She had water, but unless she found something in the church, she would have to make do with that for now. The baby was a bit fussy, and Courtney knew she had to be hungry. She rocked her gently in her arms until she fell back asleep. She looked around, wondering if she should explore the rest of the church or work on getting the boat out of the window first. The boat was secured with the rope, so it would not float away, even if the church settled and it was somehow dislodged from the window. Since the sun was not completely up, she decided to explore the church first. Not wanting to take a chance with the baby, she put the sleeping infant back in her seat, tucking the blanket around her after she had buckled her in securely. Soon they would be fellow passengers aboard their little boat, but right now she had to see if the church offered any supplies.

She went down the steps to the platform, wading through the shallow water, and headed down the center of the sanctuary. Going through the door, she made her way around to another part of the church. The water was not as deep here, so the church must have tipped a bit when the storm hit. Courtney saw a small cafeteria that had a counter with places for coffee and teapots. Above the counter was a sign that read, *Then Jesus said to them, "I am the bread of life. He who comes to Me shall never hunger, and he who believes in Me shall never thirst." John 6:35.* If only that were true, Courtney thought to herself, feeling more hungry and thirsty than she had ever been in her life.

There was a sink off to the side, and she looked in awe at what stood in the corner. A refrigerator! She made her way quickly to the refrigerator and opened the door. It was still cool inside, and she found several items she could use: bottles of water, a container of leftover fruit and vegetable pieces, and another of tiny sandwiches that looked like they had been part of a party tray. There was also a can of coffee and creamer and a small bag of donut holes.

Courtney set the water and the two containers of leftovers on the counter and closed the door. At the last minute, she opened it back up and snatched the donut holes. Popping a couple in her mouth, she chewed hungrily as she moved on to the cupboards over the sink. The first one had salt and pepper and various spices and mixes. Disappointed, she opened the next cupboard and found plastic bags, paper plates, and napkins. Grabbing one of the larger plastic bags, she placed her findings inside and headed back the way she had come, brushing donut crumbs off her face, worried that the tiny baby would wake. As she started to make her way back into the sanctuary, she noticed a small room across the hall labeled *Cry Room*. Turning back, she went into the room.

The room held a small crib and a large tub of baby toys. There was a rocking chair that had slid into one corner and a changing table along one wall. Above the changing table someone had painted another verse: *Train up a child in the way he should go, And when he is old he will not depart from it. Proverbs 22:6.* Courtney shook off the feeling that these verses were some kind of message. She pushed away her memories of the night in the park when she had begged God to help her, including the whisper she vaguely remembered hearing *I am here* at the playground.

Excited about finding a room that was obviously used to care for infants, she opened the doors under the changing table. Inside she found diapers in several sizes, baby wipes, and various jars of baby food all jumbled together. She knew the infant she had found was too young for baby food, but as she pushed the jars to the side, she saw several canisters of instant formula. Picking one up and looking at the label, she saw that this one was for infants from six to twelve months. Setting it down and reaching for the other canister, she again read the label: *From birth to six months.* Hurray! She had food for the baby and food for herself. She added the formula to her bag, knowing she could make the baby a bottle immediately. Reaching back inside, she took a stack of diapers that looked the smallest, hoping they would fit. Standing up, she added those to her bag as well, along with a thick package of baby wipes. The little girl would be fed and dry, at least for now.

Courtney made her way back to the platform and set her treasures down. The baby's eyes were open, and she started to fuss when she saw Courtney pick up the baby bottle that was tucked in her seat. Carefully Courtney rinsed out the bottle with some of the water. She put a scoop of the powder in the bottle, added water to the eight-ounce mark on the side as the directions instructed, and shook the bottle until the powder dissolved completely. The baby started to cry in earnest. Courtney set the bottle down and unbuckled the hungry baby, settling her in the crook of her elbow. She knew the formula was cold, but the baby didn't seem to mind and sucked the nipple hungrily.

Once the baby was fed and changed, Courtney placed her on the big blanket she had used the night before and used some of the wipes to clean the baby seat. As she was wiping down the plastic pad inside the seat, she noticed a small zipped plastic bag that had slipped beneath the pad. Pulling it out, she saw a note inside. Excited to think there might be information about the baby's family, she opened the bag immediately. The note was not information about the baby. It simply said, *Please save my baby. I have no way to take care of her. I am lost and alone and there is no one who can help me. I don't want to live like this anymore, but it's not her fault. Please make sure she has a decent life. Tell her I'm sorry.*

Courtney read the note twice and turned it over to make sure there was nothing else. Shocked that anyone could be hurting enough to want to die, she replaced the note in the bag and stuck it in her pocket, more determined than ever to save this baby. Sadness threatened to overwhelm her, until she remembered the effort made to keep the baby alive. She thought about the life jacket and plastic bag, the diapers and bottle. This baby's mom had done everything she could think of to give her a chance. Courtney picked up the baby and hugged her close before she put her back in the seat and buckled her in. She was the only one left to keep her safe! She rocked the seat gently until the baby fell asleep. She ate a couple of the small sandwiches and some of the fruit, then washed it down with a bottle of the water. More determined than ever, she got to work loosening the boat from the window.

She pulled open the tool bag that she had salvaged. Inside she found a sturdy hammer, which she pulled out and tried to wipe free of mud. Moving over to the window, she surveyed the problem. The boat had wedged tightly in the opening, which was almost level with the water outside. Courtney knew if the water continued to rise, it was only a matter of time before the water would overrun the window and flow into the church—one more reason to get the boat loose and be on their way.

Using the pry end of the hammer, Courtney began the task of tearing away the window frame to make room to push the boat out of the window. The frame had been damaged when the windows blew out, but pulling out the rest of the frame was still hard work. After getting one side removed, she could see that she was making headway. Anxiously, she started on the other side, watching over her shoulder, and noticed that the noise had woken the baby, who was watching her with her bright-blue eyes. Continuing on the other side of the window, she was rewarded with movement of the boat as the frame gave way and came out of the window with a loud screech.

By wiggling the end of the boat that still protruded through the window, Courtney was able to make progress pushing it out of the window. With a mighty shove she pushed it free. It was held in place by the rope that Courtney had secured it with the night before. Making sure the rope still held the boat securely, she began gathering their new supplies. She smiled when she noticed the infant had her little fist in her mouth, sucking it contentedly.

Taking the bag of food and baby supplies in one hand, Courtney stepped up on the windowsill and jumped lightly into the waiting boat. The boat dipped a bit at the movement, but Courtney was a small girl, so the movement was minimal. Now she had to go back in the church and do it again with the baby. Taking care to tuck the blanket around the little girl and make sure she was securely fastened in the seat, she made her way back to the window. Looking back to make sure she had gotten everything, she noticed the verse on the wall again: *For by grace you have been saved through faith, and that not of yourselves; it is the gift of God. Ephesians 2:8.*

Thinking about the note from the baby's mother had given Courtney a new perspective. Or maybe this whole experience had matured her. Regardless, the church reminded her of God and how much her relationship with Him had meant. She felt like He was there with her, leading her. An overwhelming sense of regret and thankfulness came over her, making her do something that she hadn't done for many years. She bowed her head and thanked God for looking after her, for helping her rescue the baby, and for providing a place for them to rest and gather the supplies they needed to survive. Tears trickled down her cheeks as she remembered praying at night with her daddy as a little girl. Maybe it was the stress of the situation or the verses on the walls of the church or the little girl who now depended on her, but for the first time in a long time, she thought about her faith as a positive thing. Heaving a sigh of relief and gripping the baby seat tightly, she stepped into the window and jumped into the waiting boat.

Chapter 5

Courtney's arms were sore from rowing the boat, but today she could hear sirens again and she thought the land in the distance was getting closer. Ignoring the pain in her arms, Courtney began to sing a silly childhood song about rowing. She smiled at the baby as she sang.

They passed more debris and made their way around several obstacles. As the sun rose high in the sky, Courtney once again made a small tent over the sleeping baby to protect her from the sun. She had paused her rowing to feed her the rest of the bottle and change her again. Now she seemed to be sleeping peacefully. Courtney chugged a bottle of water herself and ate the rest of the donut holes. It was time to move on.

She had rowed for what seemed like hours when she rounded a curve in the water and saw help directly in front of her. It looked like a large platform rising up out of the water, and people covered the surface. A large motor boat had pulled up near the platform, which Courtney saw was actually the flat roof of a large warehouse of some kind. Before she could take it all in, someone spotted her and began shouting and waving his arms. Courtney quickly made her way to the side of the roof. The noise woke the baby, and she started to cry. Courtney pulled the blanket loose to check on the baby, rocking the seat to calm her.

"She has a baby!" someone shouted. An older gentleman knelt down at the edge of the roof, reaching a hand down to Courtney.

"Let me help you, young lady," he said kindly. "Is your baby okay?"

"Yes, I think so," Courtney said shyly, handing the man the rope that was still attached to one end of the boat. Once he held the boat close, she handed the baby seat up to the man. She quickly gathered up the bag of supplies that she had left and turned back to the man who was reaching down to give her a hand. A teenage boy held on to the rope, and she could see the baby seat right beside him. More concerned about the infant than herself, Courtney took his hand and stepped onto the platform. As soon as she was safely on the roof, she picked up the baby seat with her free hand.

People were everywhere. Some were quiet, some were crying, some were still in shock. Standing next to the older gentleman who had helped her aboard, Courtney turned to him. "What's happening?" she asked him. "Is help coming?"

"All we know is they are supposed to be sending help. They are taking as many as possible to a shelter on the outskirts of Georgia, but it is a slow process and more than an hour away. By the way, I'm John," the man offered. His forehead wrinkled, and he scratched his chin as he glanced again at the baby, seeming to come to a quick decision. "Let me see if they have room for you. I know they are close to leaving."

Walking over to the waiting motorboat that was already full of people, the man spoke briefly to the person operating the boat, gesturing at Courtney and the baby. The man appeared to be saying no, pointing at the other passengers already loaded. Suddenly a woman stood up and whispered something to the man. He stopped pointing and nodded yes. She looked toward Courtney and waved.

John came back to Courtney and said they would make room for her and her baby. Courtney was so thankful she gave John a big hug. Setting the baby down, she dug through her bag, giving him the little food she had left.

"Somebody needs this more than I do," she said. "I'm sure there will be something at the shelter." John smiled his thanks, and as she made her way over to the waiting boat, he went over to an elderly couple and gave them the food.

The lady who had waved at her was waiting in the boat and stood up to take the baby seat as Courtney climbed in. She looked worriedly at the number of people huddled in the boat and squeezed in beside the lady, taking the seat and holding it on her lap. The baby looked directly at Courtney, and she patted her cheek. Satisfied, the little one closed her eyes and drifted back to sleep.

"Hi, I'm Shannon Smith," the lady said with a smile. "Girl or boy?"

"Oh, a g-girl," Courtney stammered.

"Well, she looks brand-new, and it's nice that she is young and sleeps a lot. I'm sure she will be fine. I knew we could fit you in. You are so tiny to have a little one of your own."

Courtney was startled as the siren on the boat went off. As they headed off toward the shelter, she realized it was the one she had been hearing on and off. Smiling shyly at the friendly lady, she adjusted the seat more comfortably on her lap. She was so tired, and her entire body ached. She tried to pay attention as Shannon told her about her husband and daughter, but only a small part of it registered. She just wanted to get on solid ground!

About an hour later, the boat crossed from Florida into Georgia and began making preparations to land. Courtney had watched the distant land come closer and closer until she finally saw the shoreline and several long docks jutting out into the water. Soon she could see people gathered on the shore. The passengers began collecting their few belongings and watched anxiously as the boat docked. Once the boat was tied securely, several young men started helping them step out of the boat and onto the dock.

Having been one of the last passengers aboard, Courtney was one of the first to step forward. The baby was still fast asleep as she handed the baby seat to the waiting dock hands. One of the young men passed the seat to another and reached back to help Courtney alight. Thanking him, she rushed over to reclaim the infant seat. An older woman met her at the end of the dock and directed her to a waiting bus that would take them all to the shelter. Thankful but tired, Courtney boarded the bus, wondering what lay ahead.

Chapter 6

Once all the passengers were loaded onto the bus, they began the journey to the shelter. Courtney thought about what she would be facing at the shelter, knowing from her experience with the lady on the boat that people would assume the baby was hers. She had become attached to the little one and was not ready to give her up, and she worried that no one would make sure she got a good home. What would happen to her? After thinking and rethinking her situation, she decided that her best bet would be to let them think the baby was hers and use a different name. She sat and prayed that she would be able to protect this little one.

"Dear Jesus, you came into this world under a bright star, sent by your Father to take away the sins of the world. Now I think you have sent this other little baby to me, knowing I would care for her, knowing that I needed to find you again. Please help me keep her safe and find a home and means to care for her and look for my mom. Amen." After praying, Courtney felt better, but realized she was still holding out hope that somehow her mom had survived. She touched her precious locket, feeling as if it brought her mother closer.

And now she had her new name: Star. Randomly picking a last name, she came up with "Johnson." Settling back in her seat, she smiled at the little girl who watched her with bright-blue eyes. Star Johnson seemed like a good name to her.

Almost an hour later they arrived at a long, low building with a big sign out front that said *Georgia Red Cross*. Gathering the baby and the bag that held the few supplies she had brought with her, Courtney waited her turn to exit the bus. Once on the ground, she followed the others to a door at the side of the building.

Inside, people were bustling everywhere. Partitions had been set up, with cots and small cabinets inside each cubicle. Some cubicles held multiple cots and were quite large, while others were smaller. Courtney was led to a smaller cubicle that held two small cots. Pillows and blankets were piled at the end of each cot, along with a large towel and a washcloth. The cabinet between the cots had a single door. There were basic toiletries on top of the cabinet and four bottles of water.

As a volunteer showed Courtney her space, she explained the layout of the shelter. There was an area set aside at the front of the shelter where the names of everyone in the shelter were listed. The volunteer explained that they would add her and her baby's names to the list, so families might find each other. Gently, she asked Courtney if she was looking for other family members. Knowing she must begin the charade of being a mother of a baby, Courtney shook her head and looked away. She hated being deceitful. Nodding sympathetically, the volunteer went on to tell Courtney about the shelter.

There was a first aid station, restrooms, and a shower room close to Courtney's cubicle. The lady volunteer, Sharon, went on to tell Courtney that she would be happy to tend her baby if she wanted to get a hot shower. Courtney smiled and thanked her, knowing she must look a sight after all she had gone through.

Sharon went on to tell her about the kitchen, pantry, and clothing room, telling her she was welcome to look through the clothing to find something that would fit her and the baby. A hot meal was provided at least once a day, around four in the afternoon, and sandwiches and snacks were available anytime within reason. Once she asked Courtney if she had any questions, she took down her name. Having to give her name as "Star Johnson" was uncomfortable for Courtney, but now the woman waited for the baby's name. Stammering that she had not had a chance to even name the baby yet brought a look of surprise and question to Sharon's face. Looking at her feet, she knew it sounded strange, but Courtney could not come up with a name for the little girl who had suddenly become hers. Why hadn't the baby's mom at least given her a name?

Chapter 7

Courtney was tired, and her whole body felt sore and bruised, but she decided to make the trip to the clothing room to see if they had something clean for her and the tiny infant. Once there, the volunteer who was overseeing the room came up to help Courtney. Taking Courtney over to the front corner of the room, the volunteer showed her the tiniest clothes she had ever seen. The baby was so little, but there were clothes that the woman was sure would fit her. Holding them up to the infant, Courtney agreed. Once she had what she needed for the baby, Courtney turned to leave. The volunteer stopped her, showing her a pair of leggings and a T-shirt, along with an oversized sweatshirt. At first Courtney shook her head no, thanking the woman, but as the volunteer persisted, she realized that her tattered clothing really did need replacing. As the lady put all of the clothing in the bag, she nodded discreetly toward a container that held ladies undergarments. A bit embarrassed, Courtney quickly picked out her sizes. The lady tucked them in her bag, adding a bib, bottle, and blanket for the baby. She told Courtney there were also diapers in the pantry room, near the toiletries. Realizing that she would need a few things for a shower herself, Courtney headed in that direction.

There was an elderly woman and a teenage boy helping people find what they needed in the pantry. Heading toward the toiletries, she gathered soap and shampoo and a large comb and hair ties, adding a couple of things for the baby as well and picking up a bag of diapers in the smallest size. She left the room quickly, smiling at Sharon, who had just left the room as well. They chatted as they headed toward Courtney's cubicle, and once again the woman asked if she could tend the baby while Courtney got a quick shower. Hesitantly, Courtney agreed, wanting a hot shower desperately and knowing that she must look awful.

She told Sharon she needed to get the little one changed first, then she would bring her up to the front desk. She desperately wanted to check the list of people at the shelter for her mom. She used the package of wipes to clean the baby and put on a dry diaper and sleeper. She put her back in the baby seat and carried her to the front desk. Sharon took the baby and smiled. She told Courtney they would be fine, sitting the seat right on the desk. As Courtney turned to go back to their cubicle, she spotted the list of survivors hanging on the wall. Glancing back and seeing that Sharon had turned away to talk to another volunteer about the baby, she quickly scanned the list. Her mom's name was not on the list. Disappointed, she headed back to the cubicle. After picking up what she needed, she made her way to the shower room.

Courtney had to wait a bit for a shower to open, but as soon as she went inside and turned on the hot water, she knew how much she needed it. Dressed in the comfy leggings and soft sweatshirt, she took her things back to their cubicle. After hanging her towel on a hook in her cubicle to dry, she combed her curly red hair into some kind of order, running her fingers through the curls. Anxious to retrieve the baby, she headed to the front of the center.

Courtney quickly made her way to the desk where she saw Sharon holding the infant in one arm and talking to a lady who was visibly upset. Taking the baby and thanking Sharon quietly, she rocked the baby back and forth and kissed her on the cheek before placing her back in the baby seat and heading back to their cubicle.

Tired to the bone, she fed the baby the bottle that Sharon had warmed and tucked in with her. The baby was tired and hungry too, and Courtney marveled at her ability to take a bottle whenever it was offered. Her little eyes were already starting to close as she finished the formula. Courtney quickly changed her diaper and tucked her in the cot beside her, covering them both with the blankets provided. It was chilly in the center, and snuggling the infant was comforting. Courtney was asleep almost instantly.

Despite her tired state, Courtney could not keep the nightmares at bay. Not seeing her mom's name on the survivor list had brought back the horrible memories of the fearful nights she had experienced since her mom had married Don. At first he had seemed like such a wonderful man, warm and understanding of the young girl who had lost her father. But within a couple of years, as Courtney grew up, Don had changed. Now when he put his arm around Courtney, it was always a little too tight and a little too suggestive for her comfort. Then came the first time Don had appeared behind her in the bathroom unexpectedly as she stepped out of the shower. Don had claimed it was an accident after Courtney screamed and ran hysterically to tell her mom. Courtney knew her mom didn't want to believe that Don was guilty of anything more than entering without knocking, but things had continued at an alarming rate. When Don returned home unexpectedly one evening, during a weekend that he and her mom were supposed to be away with friends, Courtney knew without a doubt what he intended. Only a timely visit from a girlfriend and her mother saved her from a confrontation with the man. He left then, but Courtney lived in fear of being cornered by the man. Even now she was fearful that somehow he had survived and was standing in the door watching her. Startled, she opened her eyes and looked around fearfully.

Once she realized it was just a dream, thoughts of her mother crept in. Could she really be dead? She thought of all they had gone through, her father's sickness and death, living alone together before her mom met Don, and all the things they had done together over her lifetime. They had been so close until Don came along. Courtney could hardly bear the thought of her mother drowning in the hurricane. If she had only come when Courtney called them! Now everything was gone! She didn't have a single picture of her. Then she thought about the locket her mother had given her. It had a tiny picture of her and her mother on one side and her mother and grandmother on the other side. Feeling for the locket, she found comfort knowing they were with her as she drifted back to sleep.

Sometime in the night, the baby stirred, and Courtney buckled her into her seat and placed it on the second cot, sliding it close beside her own. Once satisfied that the baby still slept, she lay down on her own cot and fell back into a dreamless sleep.

Chapter 8

The next morning Courtney awoke to the sounds of the infant. Although she didn't cry, Courtney could tell she was awake. She had already developed a sense of awareness when it came to the baby. Sitting up, she looked over and smiled at her. Reaching over, she patted her and spoke to her soothingly.

"Good morning, little angel," she said quietly, then went to get a clean diaper for the infant. She quickly changed her and got out water and formula for a bottle. The little girl watched her every movement with her big blue eyes.

Once the baby was fed and back in her seat, Courtney brushed her own hair and picked up the toothbrush and toothpaste on the cabinet. In the ladies' room, she entered a large stall where she could take the baby seat with her while she used the facilities. Afterward, she brushed her teeth and washed her face. Looking in the mirror, she thought she looked much better than the night before, in spite of a large bruise on one cheekbone. Knowing that a lot of people had arrived throughout the night, she was anxious to check the survivor list again. She headed to the front of the shelter.

Toward the bottom of the list, the name "Don" jumped out at her. Scanning across the page to the last name column, sure enough "Dixson" verified her worst fears. Her stepfather had survived! Frantically she searched the rest of the list for her mother's name, but it was not listed. Had he only saved himself? Was he watching for her? Thank God she had used another name! She had to get out of this shelter.

She knew her bright red curls would attract Don's attention, so back in their cubicle she twisted her hair into a tight bun and wrapped a hair tie around it. She would stop back at the clothing store and see if she could find a cap to place over it. She made her way there quickly and found a small knit hat that covered most of her hair. Feeling only slightly better, she headed out to find Sharon.

Sharon sat at the front desk as she had the day before and smiled when she saw them. Courtney quickly said good morning and thanked her again for everything they had received at the shelter. Sharon reminded her that there were multiple shelters across the country doing much of the same thing. Courtney took the opportunity to ask her where the other shelters were located, knowing this shelter had to be close to capacity. Sharon pulled out a paper that listed all of the centers in other states that were setting up similar shelters, telling Courtney they would have to start sending people to the one in Tennessee soon, as this one could not handle many more. It was unfortunate, because most of the survivors were from Florida and this was the closest shelter to their homes. She had no idea that Courtney desperately wanted to get farther away from Don.

"I would be happy to move to the shelter in Tennessee," Courtney offered. "Now that we're cleaned up and have the basics, it really doesn't matter where we're located. I mean, if it would help."

"Oh honey," Sharon said, "you have no idea! I have a father and son begging to come to this shelter so they can be near the hospital where his wife is healing. I understand, but there just isn't room! I asked several others this morning, but so far no one is willing to move. There is a bus leaving first thing tomorrow morning. Would you really consider moving? It's an eight- to ten-hour trip to the other shelter."

"Of course," Courtney replied. "I don't have to be here. I can get things around and be ready to leave any time."

"The bus leaves at six thirty a.m.," Sharon answered. "It takes most of a day to get there, and they like to get there before dark. We'll provide juice and muffins in the morning and a box lunch for the trip. Oh, and here's a bag to pack your things in." She pulled a big canvas bag out from under the desk. "If you need another one, just let me know."

"Okay, we'll be ready to go." Courtney took the bag and walked away as someone else came up to the desk with a question for Sharon. Now she just had to stay out of sight until tomorrow. As tired as she still felt, she would use the time to get some extra rest before the long trip.

She heaved a sigh of relief knowing that she could put some distance between her and the man who had been a predator in her own home. She headed back to her cubicle to pack.

Back in their cubicle, she gathered their things carefully, including all of the supplies they had acquired at the shelter. She washed out the two baby bottles with some of their water and measured formula powder into each clean bottle. She placed them in the pocket of the cloth bag that Sharon had provided, along with a couple of bottles of water. Then she included clothing, diapers, and toiletries. She put the infant in a fresh sleeper and piled the rest of their soiled clothing together.

Within a few minutes they were all packed up and ready to travel. Since it was still early, Courtney went in search of the laundry facility, hoping to be able to wash and dry their laundry and get a bite to eat before they had to leave.

Watching carefully for Don, she made her way to the laundry room, where she found an empty washer and placed their soiled laundry inside. Once it was washed, she carried it to an empty dryer. After folding her clean laundry into a neat pile, she placed it on top of the baby seat and headed back to add it to their bag.

When Courtney returned to their cubicle, someone had been kind enough to leave a sandwich on her cabinet, along with an apple, a banana, and two more bottles of water. She would get breakfast and the box lunch in the morning for the bus ride, so this would do for today. She didn't want to risk running into Don in the cafeteria. Exhausted with all that had happened, she ate the sandwich and banana. Seeing the little one was sound asleep again, she lay down to rest. As always, thoughts of her mom ran over and over in her mind: her mom baking cookies, her mom fixing her hair, and her mom beaming at her last choir recital. Could she really leave her mom behind? Maybe she could continue to call Sharon and ask her if her mom's name showed up on the survivor list. She could always be anonymous. Sharon probably wouldn't even remember her anyway, considering all the survivors she met every day. Feeling better, and still recovering from her ordeal, Courtney slept.

Early the next morning Courtney was apprehensive, but breathed easier when she saw her bus pull up outside the shelter. Picking up her bag with one hand and holding tightly to the baby seat with the other hand, she didn't notice that her hat had slipped to one side, letting loose some of the curls that had escaped her bun. She found a seat and settled in for the long trip to Tennessee.

Someone else did notice, however. He stood in the shadows just outside the shelter watching the familiar figure board the bus, surprised at the baby seat, but pretty certain about the girl.

Chapter 9

Courtney rode along with the baby on the seat beside her, feeling like she had dodged a bullet. The baby slept peacefully, and she was finally able to relax. Once she got to the shelter in Tennessee, she would ask about temporary housing, employment, etc. She would need to apply for a copy of her birth certificate and a new driver's license and thought she could probably find a library and do most of it online.

The hurricane had come on November 30, so it must be the first week of December. She would be seventeen soon. She felt much older. She was going to have to figure out a way to support herself and this infant, and she needed to do it as soon as possible. She had more than herself to think about now.

She knew she had a full day of travel to get to the shelter in Tennessee. Since the baby was still sleeping, she ate her muffin and drank her juice, then decided a nap was in order. In an effort to protect the infant, she placed her seat on the side nearest the window, putting herself on the aisle and draping a blanket over the seat so no one would bother or even see the baby. She rested her feet on the bag of their belongings, letting her head lean back against the seat and over toward the infant.

It was still dark outside, so sleep came easily. Suddenly, Courtney was afraid. Her thin summer nightshirt fluttered up around her, but Courtney was in bed and there shouldn't be air fluttering there. Then she realized that she was not alone. A large shadow at the door moved closer, and she felt his weight as he sat on the bed. She tried to scream, but something was covering her face and no sound would come out. As he reached for her, she tried to scream again with all her might. The low growl that was forced from her throat woke her up.

Pushing the baby blanket away from her face, she realized she had fallen toward the baby seat as she slept, and the blanket had slipped over her face. Heart beating like crazy, she sat up straight and looked out of the window. *Thank God it was only another nightmare. Not real, not real*, she kept repeating to herself. Would she ever rid herself of that horrible man?

Courtney thought about all she had learned about Mr. Donald Arnold Dixson (aka Kurtis). He was not the nice man her mother thought him to be. Why couldn't her mom have seen through his fake kindness and discovered the evil man who lurked beneath? Admittedly, she hadn't seen it at first either.

He had been wanted for murder in Colorado but had gotten off on a technicality. The story Courtney uncovered online used the name Donald A. Kurtis, but there was a grainy picture of him that she was convinced was Don. The woman who accused him, his wife at the time, had claimed that Don had killed her daughter and had proof that he had been terrorizing her before her death, which had been ruled a suicide. She described him as a predator, preying on single women with teenage daughters who were vulnerable. Unfortunately she had a car accident during the early stages of the trial and went over a mountain cliff. Neither the woman's phone, nor any other evidence, could be recovered. With nothing left to point to Don having anything to do with it, the case was eventually dropped. At least his story about being widowed was true. However, Courtney found several articles written at the time of the trial that pointed toward Don being a murderer, including one from the girl's best friend, who had verified that Don had been terrorizing the girl. He lost his job and eventually left the state, but a lot of people thought he was guilty of both murders.

Courtney had just discovered all this the weekend before the hurricane hit. She had started locking her door at night and staying with her friend Maddison whenever she could. She had wanted to tell her mom what she had discovered, but the storm had come before she had the chance. Maybe it was better this way. Tears filled her eyes, brimming over in spite of herself. She missed her mom so much!

Tired of her own thoughts, Courtney pulled out the small Bible that Sharon had pressed into her hand before she left. She had tucked it into her sweatshirt pocket without thinking. Now she took it out, finding comfort in the small book that had once meant so much to her. Her thoughts turned to her father and mother. Courtney's parents had been strong in their faith.

Courtney had been raised to believe in God and eternal salvation. At the young age of eight, Courtney had given her heart to the Lord. She had stood on the platform next to her dad, saying bravely that she believed that God had sent his only Son, Jesus Christ, to die for our sins and she believed in Him and life everlasting. She had stepped into the baptismal pool and been baptized in the name of the Father, Son, and Holy Ghost. She would never forget the experience and never forget that she had believed with all her heart. Two short years later, her father fell ill. After three long years battling cancer, he finally died. "I am not afraid of death," he told his young daughter, "I am going to meet Jesus!"

Courtney and her mom had been at her father's side throughout his cancer, chemo, and all the rest. They had prayed incessantly to God, asking Him to heal the man they loved with all their hearts and make him whole again. Courtney had promised everything she could think of if God would only make him well. But her prayers were not answered. Her father still suffered . . . still died. At his funeral, Courtney, in her overwhelming grief, vowed to never pray again. Her mother told her it was foolish to blame God, but she persisted.

Looking back now, she realized her mother was right. God couldn't stop human illness. He couldn't stop the choices people made that led to their demise. He was still the loving Father she had learned about as a child and prayed to during the storm. And after that night, she knew he was still there. Still waiting for her to come back to her faith and believe once again. God never gives up on His children.

Courtney thought about the church she had found after the storm. Surely that had not been a coincidence. The verses on the walls had spoken to her, reinforced what she had known all along. Her God was a pure and loving God, and He was there for her—always. She was ready to accept it all once more. She knew her mother would be proud of her decision, if only she were here.

As she leafed through the little Bible, she found the book of Proverbs. Looking more carefully, she realized she had missed reading her Bible, and now that precious Bible that her parents had presented her upon her baptism was gone, lost in the storm. Still thumbing through the pages, she stopped when a particular verse stood out to her. She read Proverbs 31:25–26 (NLT): *She is clothed with strength and dignity, and she laughs without fear of the future. When she speaks, her words are wise, and she gives instructions with kindness.* She stopped and thought about those words. Was God speaking to her once again? Could she follow His words and become all God wanted her to be?

Oh, she hoped she could! She could not really imagine laughing without fear of the future right now, but she could use this Bible and try to live with integrity going forward. Looking down at the infant beside her, she promised herself and this sweet little baby girl to give it a try.

"Help me God," she prayed. "Help me to be that woman described in the book of Proverbs. I want to be like her, and I want to trust in you again. Amen."

When the bus finally arrived in Tennessee, Courtney alighted with new hope in her heart. This could be a new start for her and this little baby God had entrusted her with. As if she knew Courtney was thinking about her, the baby stirred and opened her big blue eyes.

"Don't you worry, little one. I will watch over you and keep you safe."

Chapter 10

Having gathered the basic necessities at the other shelter, Courtney quickly settled her and the baby's things into their living quarters, arranging everything in the space provided.

Although it was larger, the layout was quite similar to the other shelter they had stayed in. She had followed her assigned volunteer, who introduced herself as Carly, to a similar cubicle set up toward the back of the shelter the night before. It was a little bigger than the one Courtney had stayed in previously, and to her surprise they had put a large rocking chair in one corner for her to rock the baby. Carly smiled at her delight with the chair, accepting her thanks as she began going over the shelter's facilities, much as Sharon had gone over them with her at the shelter in Georgia. Courtney was a little more comfortable with her new name now and decided to use her middle name, Grace, for the infant. It was just too weird for her not to have a name!

She changed "Grace" and made her another bottle. The little girl had sucked happily on the bottle as she rocked her gently in the rocking chair. She couldn't help singing softly as she devoured the bottle. Courtney's heart melted as Grace's tiny fingers wrapped tightly around one of hers. Tired from the long journey, they went to bed early.

Courtney woke up excited to check everything out at the new shelter. Today, after feeding and changing the hungry, wet baby, Courtney carried the now-content infant with her to wash out the bottle in the ladies' room. She ran into the volunteer she had met the night before, who begged to hold the infant for a moment. Courtney took the time to use the facilities and wash her hands. As she took Grace from the volunteer, Carly mentioned that she had seen a baby sling in the clothing room. She told Courtney she thought it would come in handy for securing her when Courtney needed her hands free. Thanking her, Courtney went in search of the clothing room.

The baby sling was exactly what Courtney needed, and Grace seemed content to snuggle up against her whether awake or sleeping. After being able to use both hands during breakfast, she was amazed at how much she liked it too. It allowed Courtney to do a little more exploring at the shelter. She discovered a pantry with snacks, a water cupboard with an unlimited supply of bottles of water, and a medical clinic. Her exploring also uncovered a small library, where people had donated books of all kinds. Thinking that she would have to come back to it, she left the room and headed toward the front of the shelter, where she knew she would find lists of names of people at the center, classes that were being offered, and a sign-up sheet for seeing a doctor. Going immediately to the list of names, in spite of knowing that it was very unlikely that her mother would have made it this far, she noticed her name toward the bottom: Star Johnson and infant daughter, Grace. Looking through the list and satisfied there was no one she knew, she went on to the other lists.

Deciding that it couldn't hurt to take a class on writing a resume and one on infant care, she quickly signed up for both and headed back to the library. Courtney had always been an avid reader, even as a young child. Searching through shelves of books, after noticing that Grace was once again sound asleep, Courtney found a paperback novel that she thought looked interesting. Continuing to another shelf, she also found a colorful book on infants and decided that might be a good one to borrow. As she was heading to the front of the room to ask about checking them out, a leather-bound book at the end of a shelf caught her eye. It was a dark teal color and simply said *Holy Bible*. There were ferns around the title in a shiny gold color, and Courtney thought it was one of the prettiest Bibles she had ever seen. Fingering the cover made her wish again for the Bible her parents had given her, now lost in the hurricane.

Turning back toward the woman sitting at the front of the room, Courtney inquired about checking out the books.

"Oh, you don't have to check them out," the woman told her. "People have donated these books for others who want them. Just take the ones you want. If you decide you don't want to keep them for yourself, just bring them back when you are done reading them and put them back on the shelf."

"Wow, thank you so much," Courtney said.

"No problem." The woman pulled out a small bag for the two books Courtney had selected. "Are you sure you don't want the Bible? It's so pretty and seems so lost sitting there without an owner."

Courtney found herself going back for the Bible. "You know, I think I will take it," she said. "It really is lovely. I have a very small one that I will bring back and put on the shelf for someone else. Thanks again."

As the woman added the Bible to her bag, Courtney felt a bit of excitement at owning such a beautiful Bible and couldn't wait to make it her own. It would help erase a tiny bit of the regret she felt about the one she had lost.

Going back to her room, she placed the baby back in her baby seat for the rest of her nap and stretched out on her own bed to look at her treasures. Unable to resist the pretty teal Bible, she opened that first. Someone had left a small bookmark in the book of Psalms. Moving the bookmark, she read the verse that someone had highlighted, Psalm 23:6: *Surely goodness and mercy shall follow me all the days of my life; and I will dwell in the house of the LORD forever.* It sounded so easy, and Courtney remembered a time when it had been. She made up her mind on the spot that she would find something to pray about every night. God was surely the one who had saved her from the hurricane, brought her the tiny infant, and helped her to find shelter and get away from Don. She was ready to let God know how thankful she was.

After leafing through the book on infants and reading a chapter of the novel, Courtney's eyes grew heavy and she decided to take a nap herself. Checking to make sure Grace was still asleep, once again she pulled the cot with the baby seat on it close to her own and closed her eyes.

Chapter 11

Courtney awoke to the baby stirring. She knew she must be wet and hungry again, so she quickly roused herself to take care of the child. Once the infant was changed and fed, she realized she had slept the day away and it was almost time for the hot meal. Fitting the baby into the sling, Courtney headed to the cafeteria.

While Courtney was eating, a young girl came and sat beside her, placing her tray of food in front of her not far from Courtney's. She looked over at Courtney with a smile and said hello.

"My name is Zoey" she said quietly. "Your baby is really sweet."

"Thank you," Courtney replied. "I'm S-Starr." She stammered a bit using the unfamiliar name, but gave the girl a smile to cover it. "Are you alone?"

Tears welled up in the girl's eyes and trickled down her cheeks. "I am," the girl replied, obviously choked up. "I lost my parents in the hurricane. The shelter in Georgia is full now, so they sent me here. My grandparents are on their way to get me, but they are driving from a town in northern Kentucky and they have to go slow. It will probably be a couple of days before they get here. Pops has trouble seeing at night, so they can only travel during daylight."

Courtney felt immediate sympathy for the young girl. She scooted over to Zoey, baby and all, and tried to give her a quick hug. "I'm so sorry," she said. "I think I lost my mom too. I have been checking the survivor lists at the shelters. Nothing so far, so I'm pretty sure she's gone."

The girls bonded instantly, knowing exactly how the other felt.

"Please, eat your food while it's hot," Courtney continued. "It's really good."

Zoey tried valiantly to eat some of the chicken and potatoes in front of her, managing about half of it. They chatted about the things at the shelter, discovering that their sleeping areas were very close. Courtney tried to stay away from the painful reminder of the loss of the girl's parents by asking her about her age and interests instead. She told Zoey about the library and offered to go with her after their meal to see if she could find a couple of books. They were only a year apart in age, and both girls shared a love of reading, so they definitely had some things in common. Courtney told her about the books she had discovered that day, and the fact that they were free. They left the cafeteria on a more hopeful note.

In the library the girls actually had fun looking for books Zoey would enjoy. After she selected a couple, Courtney invited her back to her room to see the ones she had picked out. She knew Zoey was curious about the baby, but Courtney was reluctant to tell her all of the circumstances. Instead, when asked about her dad, she opened up a bit about the whole experience with his illness and death. Naturally, this led to a discussion about her stepdad, Don, and she found herself telling her about her fears of him and what she had discovered about his past. Zoey agreed that the whole situation seemed off, and Courtney felt like she had made a true friend that day. They had both had to face hardship and being alone, and now they had each other. It was an instant bond.

Zoey offered to feed Grace while Courtney took a shower that night, so Courtney made her a bottle, changed the baby, and handed her off to Zoey in the rocking chair. Zoey smiled at the little girl, seeming to be very comfortable feeding her. Courtney stopped and picked out some leggings and a tunic, similar to what she had found at the other shelter, took a quick shower, and came back to find both Zoey and the infant dozing in the chair.

When it came time to say good night, Courtney could tell that Zoey did not want to leave. "You can stay here with us tonight if you want to," Courtney told the girl.

The relief on Zoey's face said it all. They put the sleeping baby back in her seat, setting it on the wide stand between the two cots. Zoey made a quick trip to her room to change into more comfortable clothes and to get her own blankets, but she was back in a flash. It would be so nice to have someone to talk to and just to know that someone else was there.

As the baby slept on, the girls chatted quietly. Zoey told her about the horrific experience of watching her parents drown and be swept away by the hurricane.

"My mom insisted I have a life jacket on, and it saved my life. Unfortunately mom and dad couldn't get theirs on in time." Zoey's lip trembled as she continued. "They couldn't fight the strength of the water and kept going under. Then they just didn't come back up, and I was left by myself until I was rescued by a helicopter and brought to the shelter." Tears were falling freely now, but Zoey said it felt better to just tell someone about it.

All Courtney could do was nod in sympathy and try not to cry. Then she shared her experience with Zoey as well, and she found it comforting to talk to someone who, until today, had been a stranger. She described watching her mom and Don being swept away, running to the park, and tying herself to the tower pole. She even mentioned praying for God's help. She told Zoey about the boat and getting stuck at the church. Then, given everything they had already shared, she decided to share how she had rescued the baby. At that point, Zoey stopped her.

"Wait!" the girl cried. "The baby isn't yours?"

"Shhhh," Courtney said in a whisper. "Nobody knows." She went on to tell Zoey about the note she found with the baby. "I still keep searching the lists to see if anyone is looking for a newborn, but after finding the note, I don't think there is anyone looking for her. People keep assuming she's mine, so I just don't say anything. I can't tell people that her mother wanted to die and sent her out on her own during the hurricane! Besides, God brought her to me, I'm sure of it. I have to keep her safe."

"Oh my gosh," Zoey whispered. "Oh my gosh!"

"Please promise me you won't tell," Courtney said in despair. "She needs me, I can feel it. Besides, I know God was with me out there and sent her to me for safekeeping. And you may as well know, my name isn't Star. It's Courtney. I had to change it so Don wouldn't find me. But you can't say anything!"

"Of course I won't say anything!" Zoey answered back in a whisper herself. "Of course I won't. But it could take years to get all of this mess from the hurricane sorted out. What if nobody ever comes forward to claim the baby?"

"Then I'll keep her and raise her," Courtney said with determination. "She and I are in this together. She doesn't have anyone else, and she's counting on me. She isn't very old, and there was no name on the note I found, so I have started calling her Grace, my middle name."

"Wow!" was all Zoey could manage.

"Let's get some sleep now," Courtney suggested. "This little one will want a bottle soon."

"Okay," Zoey replied sleepily. "Thanks again for letting me stay with you. This is so much better than being alone. Good night."

"Good night, Zoey."

Courtney lay on her narrow cot thinking about the day's events. While she was happy to have found a friend to share with and confide in, she knew it added new risk to the equation. Still, she felt like she could trust Zoey. She decided this would be her topic of prayer for today.

"Dear God," she started. "Thank you for helping me find a new friend today. Thank you for the books, especially the new Bible. I believe you are there God, and I am sorry I pushed you away when my father died. Please forgive me my childish ways. Help me to be stronger and guide me in caring for this little baby you placed in my path. Help me to find ways to be pleasing to you and to use your Word going forward. And, God, please comfort Zoey as she grieves the loss of her parents. Guide her grandparents to find her and take her home and love her. I ask these things in your name, Lord. Amen."

Feeling good about remembering to pray, Courtney thought about all that had happened that day. Meeting Zoey made such a difference. Having a friend so close to her own age, and being able to talk truthfully about everything that had happened relieved some of the stress she had been dealing with. Optimistic about the days to come, she closed her eyes and slept.

Sometime in the night, the baby stirred, and Courtney got up quietly and fixed her another bottle. Glancing over at the cot where Zoey lay curled up with her blanket, Courtney smiled. Sitting in the rocking chair, she rocked quietly as she fed the baby. She thought about everything she had shared with Zoey, a complete stranger. Only she didn't seem like a stranger at all. They had so much in common and had bonded almost instantly. It felt like one more instance where God wanted her to know He was there, providing exactly what she needed.

Soon Grace's little eyes drooped, and as the last of the bottle disappeared, she fell back asleep. Placing her back in her baby seat and buckling her securely, Courtney put a soft blanket over her and crawled back into her own bed. Her very last thought before she fell asleep was, *God is good—no, God is great!*

Chapter 12

Courtney awoke and immediately checked on the baby. Seeing the infant still fast asleep, she glanced toward Zoey to find the girl watching her. They smiled at each other and whispered good morning. *How nice to have a friend again*, Courtney thought. She hadn't realized how lonely she felt until Zoey came along.

After changing and feeding the baby and getting some breakfast themselves, the girls took the infant to the shower room. Zoey needed to shower today, so she offered to take the baby in with her for a few minutes, soap her down, and pass her out to Courtney. They headed to the shower room with extra clothes and baby soap for the infant.

When they got to the shower room, they found a small baby tub leaning against one wall, so they quickly filled it with warm water, got the infant undressed, and laid her in the warm tub. To both girls' surprise, the baby loved the warm water. She squirmed a bit when Courtney put baby soap on a warm washcloth and gently washed her all over. She didn't mind when Zoey leaned over and shampooed her hair. In fact, she smiled and kicked her feet. Once the little one was thoroughly rinsed, Zoey dumped the water and jumped into a shower herself, leaving Courtney to dress the baby in a clean diaper, T-shirt, and sleeper. The little one snuggled on Courtney's shoulder until she dozed.

Courtney called out to Zoey that she was heading back to the room.

"Okay, I'll see you in a few minutes," Zoey replied.

Courtney was sitting in the rocking chair, rocking and humming as the baby slept in her arms. Zoey walked in and smiled, then settled on one of the cots and picked up the Bible that Courtney had gotten only the day before. "What a pretty Bible," Zoey commented. "Do you believe in God, Courtney?"

Courtney was taken by surprise at the innocent question and the ease with which the girl seemed to switch to her real name. She was quiet a moment before she answered her. Accepting her faith again after all these years had been difficult at times, but she felt like God had spoken to her and was back in her heart. She wanted to share how that had changed her with her new friend. Maybe it would help her to understand the whole baby situation.

"Yes, I believe in God," Courtney started hesitantly. "But I didn't until the storm. I had turned away from God when my father died because I wanted to blame him for not saving my dad. Then, during the storm I asked for God's help, and I survived. After the baby floated up to my boat and I rescued her, and we got stuck in the window of a church where the verses on the walls seemed to be speaking to me, I realized it was God trying to get my attention. I found food, water, formula, and diapers for the baby, all in this church that I had literally run right into. It had to be God, right?"

Zoey looked at Courtney in awe. "Wow! I don't know. I mean, I went to church and Sunday school with my parents over the years, but I didn't get baptized or anything. I don't think God ever talked to me that I know of, but I've never talked to God either. Have you?"

As Zoey leafed through the Bible, Courtney felt the answers come easily. "Yeah, I did a lot when I was younger, even when my dad was really sick. But when he died, I was really angry, and I stopped talking to Him and stopped praying. I've started again now, and I can't really explain it, but it just feels right." Courtney paused again as she adjusted Grace more comfortably in her arms. Then she continued, "You know, talking about all this helps. There are verses in the Bible that help you understand about God. So I picked up that pretty Bible yesterday and decided I'm going to go back to learning more about Him again. It brings me comfort thinking He's watching over me. Does any of that make sense?"

"Well," Zoey answered, "it sounds sensible. I sure would like to feel like someone was there with me right now too. Do you think we could find another Bible and learn together?"

"Absolutely," Courtney replied. "And if we don't find another Bible that you like, I know there's a little one that I left there that came from the other shelter I stayed in. You can always have that one, if it's still there. Why don't you get the rest of your things and move in with me and Grace. I mean, if you want to."

Zoey jumped up off the bed, carefully laid the Bible down, and rushed over to give Courtney and the baby and even the rocking chair an awkward hug. "I'll be right back," she told Courtney.

Courtney smiled as she watched Zoey leave to get her things. At that moment she was happy she had seen Don's name and come to this shelter. Everything was so much better now. She kissed Zoeyl on the forehead as she slept and felt some warmth creep back into her heart.

Chapter 13

Courtney and Zoey became fast friends and went everywhere together. With two of them, taking care of the baby was so much easier and their friendship grew stronger every day. Not only did they find a Bible for Zoey, but the lady in the library told them about a Bible study that was held once a week. Daycare was provided, so the girls could have a break for an hour or so and spend some time together getting to know more about God. Courtney was working on a resume, after attending the resume class, and was feeling better about finding employment. They watched the notes and survivor list every day, but there was still no sign of Courtney's mom and no one looking for a female infant.

Although it was hard to let go of the baby, even for an hour, the girls thoroughly enjoyed the Bible study. People shared their favorite verses and the girls wrote down some of the ones they liked and vowed to look them up later. Everything was going great, and the girls almost forgot where they were and what had brought them together.

They were quickly reminded when Zoey got a call a couple of days later. A woman came and got her to take the call. It was her grandparents, and they would be at the shelter the next day to pick her up. The very next day!

Courtney and Zoey were very quiet after the call. They went back to their room and just looked at each other. It was time for the baby to have another bottle, so Courtney went through the process of fixing it and settled down in the rocking chair to feed the baby. She thought even the baby must feel the heaviness hanging in the air. Finally Zoey broke the silence.

"I have an idea," she said quietly to Courtney. "Come with me."

"What!" Courtney replied. "Do you really think your grandparents would go for that?"

"Yes, I do. They have always been very loving and supportive of family. And they have a big house with bedrooms that don't even get used. If I talk to them and explain the situation, I'm sure they won't mind."

"But what do I do about Grace?" Courtney nodded at the sleeping infant. "You know I have to take her, have to pretend she's mine. What will they think about a girl with a baby at my age?"

"Well, we'll just let them think that you are older or that she is your little sister or something. We have to come up with something, Courtney!" There was desperation in Zoey's voice now, even fear.

"It'll be okay, Zoey. We'll think of something, but I can't outright lie."

Courtney walked over to the baby seat and buckled Grace back in. Sitting down on the bed, she put her arm around the younger girl, giving her a squeeze. The two girls had become such good friends, and it had been effortless. She was convinced it had to do with the difficult situations they both had faced. Courtney wanted to stay together as bad as Zoey did and thought they could continue to help each other grow and heal from all that had happened. Looking at the infant sleeping peacefully unaware in her baby seat, she hoped they could find a way to all stay together. Spotting the pretty teal Bible near the base of the baby's seat she had an idea.

"Zoey," she said to the disheartened girl beside her. "Let's pray to God for an answer."

"What," Zoey replied. "How do we do that? You know I'm not good at it yet."

"I don't think God cares about how good or bad you are at praying," Courtney answered her. "I think He wants to know our desires and even our fears. Remember that man in the Bible study who read the verse about taking everything to God? What was that verse? Did you write that one down?"

"Yeah, I think I did," Zoey replied. Reaching under the cot, she got her own Bible that still felt awkward in her hands. Pulling out the paper she had saved from the Bible study, she looked at what she had written. "Here it is," she said excitedly. "Be anxious for nothing, but in everything by prayer and supplication, with thanksgiving, let your requests be made known to God. Philippians 4:6." She looked at Courtney with big eyes.

"That's it," Courtney replied. "We need to ask God for help and then accept what happens as His will."

"But what if we don't get an answer?" Zoey asked with anxiety in her voice. "What if He doesn't answer us before my grandparents get here tomorrow?"

"We'll let Him know our situation, even though He probably already knows. Let's just pray and give it to Him, okay?"

"Okay," Zoey said doubtfully. "What do we say?"

"Why don't I start, and you can add anything I leave out, okay?" Courtney looked at the other girl, who nodded her head.

Both girls folded their hands, closed their eyes, and bowed their heads.

"Dear God," Courtney started, "thank you for bringing us together. Zoey and I come before you, knowing that we are new to prayer, but we want to learn more. We understand that you know our hearts and hear our prayers, and we'll try to accept whatever happens as your will for us. I know I haven't done that in the past, God, but I'll try harder because I want you in my life and I know you have been there. I feel the Holy Spirit inside me again, and it gives me hope." Courtney took her time, still a bit afraid of her ability to pray and say the right things to God.

Unexpectedly, Zoey chimed in. "God," she said shakily, "I haven't prayed before, except at night as a young child when my parents said my prayers with me. I don't even know completely what faith is all about. But somehow, I know in my heart that you brought us together to help each other. . . to comfort each other. I already love her, God, just like a sister. I don't want to leave her and Grace. I realize that this might not make sense, but I promise, God, if you can help us figure out a way to stay together, I will be so thankful." She paused, with tears welling up in her eyes.

Wow! Zoey was catching on quickly. Courtney's eyes welled up in response, but they had to finish bringing their request to God, so she went on to finish the prayer. "God, we need your help. We need to find a way to stay together when Zoey's grandparents arrive. Please show us the answer to the situation we find ourselves in. We bring this to you with much thankfulness for the time you have already given us, and we ask this all in your Son's name. Amen."

"Thank you, God. Amen." Zoey barely added her last words before she broke down and started to cry in earnest.

"It'll be okay, we've brought our request to God just like it says in the Bible. Now we have to stop being anxious and wait for an answer."

Zoey dried her tears and nodded her head. She hugged her Bible to her chest, as if comforted by the words they had prayed. By then it was time for lunch, so she put the Bible away as Courtney changed Grace and grabbed the baby sling, placing her inside. The girls headed to the cafeteria to get a salad or sandwich, familiar now with the meal schedule at the shelter.

Chapter 14

The girls tried to be cheerful for the rest of the day. They both went to the childcare class that Courtney had signed up for earlier, having fun when the instructor called them up front to illustrate the proper way to change a diaper, since they had an infant with them. The baby charmed everyone by lying there calmly as Courtney showed the class the proper way to lay the diaper and fasten the tabs on each side. They laughed when the baby seemed to smile at the end of the demonstration, and the whole class clapped.

After the class, the girls went back to the front of the shelter, looking at the list of people at the shelter and the notes that they had left for their loved ones. It was heartbreaking to read some of the messages people left, hoping to reconnect with someone they had lost. They didn't find anything about a missing female infant, although Courtney's heart almost stopped when she saw a note that read *MISSING BABY!* As she read the note, she heaved a sigh of relief when it went on to describe the baby as a boy, almost a year old. It was followed almost instantly by the horrible thought that he might have died in the storm. She prayed he hadn't, hugging Grace even closer. The hurricane had impacted so many families!

She carefully went down the entire list of names, even though she was pretty certain that Don was at the other shelter. Satisfied, the girls went to the game room, where they could relax and play a game of Scrabble.

The hot meal that night was chili, which Courtney knew was one of Zoey's favorites. The corn muffins smelled delicious, but the girls had a hard time eating because of their anxiety about the future. After the meal, they skipped the hot cherry cobbler and decided to go to the laundry room and get their soiled clothing cleaned up. They only had one batch between the three of them, so it didn't take long. When it was washed, dried, and folded, they headed back to their room for the evening. Courtney left out the clothes that she and the baby would wear to sleep in and clothes for the following day. She decided to pack up the remainder of their things so they would be ready to travel, if God answered their prayers.

Zoey was much quieter than usual as she laid out her pajamas and clothes for the next day. She packed up her few belongings as well, placing her new Bible right on top so she wouldn't forget it. Finally she turned to Courtney. "Anything?" she asked her quietly.

Courtney shook her head no but added some encouragement. "We can pray again tonight," she said. "Let's just read for a bit, until I have to feed Grace, okay?"

Zoey shook her head yes and got out the novel she was reading as Courtney got out hers. The girls read for about an hour while the baby lay on her tummy beside Courtney. They had gotten her a little stuffed bear that had a mirror on one side. Courtney had propped it up against her leg where the baby could see it, and she seemed fascinated by it. It was quiet in the room, except for an occasional baby noise.

Finally it was time to feed Grace and get her tucked in. Courtney made the bottle, but Zoey wanted to sit in the rocker and feed her since it might be the last time. Courtney wanted to encourage her that it would all work out, but she wasn't sure herself. She wondered how she would make it without Zoey, now that they had formed such a tight bond.

When the baby was burped, changed, and back in her seat for the night, the girls got ready for bed. Lying on their cots, they watched the baby drift off to sleep. Courtney finally suggested they try praying again.

"Let's do it separately," Zoey said solemnly. "Maybe we will have a better chance if we both send God the same message."

Courtney was determined not to give up this time. Her silent prayer was simple and direct: *Dear God, you know our request from yesterday. You know the desires of our hearts. Please give us a sign, or the words to say, that will keep us together tomorrow when Zoey's grandparents arrive. Thank you for all of our blessings today, the class and food and time with Grace. And, God, if the answer is that we have to separate, please help me be strong when I have to say goodbye. Amen.*

Zoey felt lost. She simply could not believe that she was going to have to leave Courtney and the baby behind. What could she say that they hadn't already said? Finally she decided to keep it short.

Dear God, I'm grateful for the time you have given me with Courtney and Grace. I love them God, and I hope you'll help us find a way to stay together. Thank you again. Amen.

Zoey couldn't face tomorrow if the answer was no, and nothing she thought about could take away her anxiety. She lay quietly crying until she fell asleep.

Courtney watched her friend in the bed across the room and could do nothing. She still had hope that something would happen to keep them together if it was meant to be. Otherwise, being the older of the two, she knew she would have to find a way to be strong and encourage Zoey to go with her grandparents.

The next morning, the girls went about their normal routine. Grace had slept the whole night through and was hungry for her bottle as soon as they could get it ready. After she was fed and changed, they took her down to the shower room for another bath. She loved the little tub of water and kicked her feet when they let her lie there for a minute. Afterward, Courtney took the baby back to their room so Zoey could shower. When she returned to the room, Courtney took her turn. She washed and dried her hair, knowing that she might not have Zoey's help in the near future. When she returned, the girls put the baby in the baby sling and headed to breakfast.

Before they could finish their breakfast, Carly came into the cafeteria, leading Zoey's grandparents, who had just arrived. Courtney could see Zoey's excitement, in spite of the tears that ran freely down all of their faces. A sense of foreboding came over her, as they still hadn't figured out a way to stay together.

Once Zoey had greeted her grandparents, she turned and introduced them to Courtney and Grace, who nestled against her in the baby sling. Her grandparents were Mary and Tom Scott. They all shook hands and sat and visited while the girls finished up their breakfast. Zoey suddenly talked like a little chatterbox after being so quiet earlier. Courtney listened as she told her grandparents how they had met, and since they already knew Zoey's story, she told them about Courtney losing her mom and running to the park to save herself. When Zoey was finally done, her grandmother reached over and patted Courtney's hand where it lay on the table.

"You are a very brave girl, young lady," she said to Courtney. "What are you going to do now?"

Courtney didn't really know what to say. She finally got her wits about her, and seeing Zoey's stricken face, she tried to smile. "I haven't really figured it all out yet," she said honestly. Her voice was a little shaky, and she tried to stay calm. "It's been wonderful having Zoey here the last few days, but I know I have to try to find some kind of housing and a job . . . and daycare." She patted the little one hanging in the sling. "I'm not sure yet what the expectations are here at the shelter, but they are helping me put a resume together." Courtney felt like she was babbling, but the words just poured out on their own.

"Well, honey, do you have any relatives or friends who can help you?" Zoey's grandpa said it gruffly, but Courtney could see the kindness and concern on his face.

"No, not really," Courtney went on. "But no worries, I'll figure it all out." Her voice sounded overly bright and cheerful, even to her.

Zoey's grandma looked down at Zoey, who was sitting between her and her husband, then looked at her husband, who nodded his head. "Look," she said to Courtney, as Zoey held her breath, "we have a big house in Kentucky with plenty of room. Would you like to stay with us for a while, until you figure out what you're going to do? I know it's not where you're from, but I'm sure Zoey would love to have your company, and it would certainly be a little easier than trying to figure it all out by yourself. We would be happy to help you if you want to come. I think Zoey will vouch for us being good people. Besides, we are still licensed for foster care, so I don't see why anyone would have a problem with it."

Zoey hugged her grandma's arm excitedly, and her smile lit up her whole face. "Please come with us," she exclaimed. "I told you they would be okay with it!"

"Are you sure?" Courtney couldn't believe that their prayers were being answered just when it seemed hopeless.

"Of course we're sure, or we wouldn't have asked." Grandpa's voice was gruff again, but he smiled. "Now let's get your things and get a move on."

Zoey's grandma nodded as the girls got up to take care of their breakfast trays. She was still reeling from the news of her daughter and son-in-law's deaths, but she had to admit that the girls made things easier. She knew it might be a handful, but she just had to help this girl and her baby. Somehow it seemed like it was the right thing to do. Besides, that was why she and Tom had become foster parents in the first place. They loved having youngsters around.

"Go help the girls with their bags, Tom," she said to her husband. "I'll go up front and tell them we are collecting our girls."

Courtney melted at the words Zoey's grandma spoke so easily. Yes, indeed, God was certainly answering their prayers. Zoey's grandpa followed the girls to their room, where they picked up the bags that were packed and ready, strapped the infant back into her seat, and headed up to find Zoey's grandma. Courtney never learned what was said or how she managed it, but before she could blink Zoey's grandma was pushing them all out the door to a big SUV that was parked in front of the building. As they got in the vehicle, Courtney's concern about there being enough room for her and the baby dissolved.

"We need to stop and get that little one a proper car seat," Courtney heard Zoey's grandma say. They stopped at the first Target store they came to, and all trooped inside to pick out a car seat for Grace. She felt a bit awkward, but they pushed her worries aside, purchased the car seat, and headed back to the vehicle. Zoey's grandpa hooked the seat into the middle of the back seat of the vehicle and made sure it was secured properly. Courtney took Grace out of the baby seat that had saved this little girl's life and handed her to Zoey's grandpa, who buckled her in. She carried the battered seat to a nearby trash can, said a silent thank-you to Grace's mom, and tossed it in.

As Zoey's grandparents got in the front, Zoey and Courtney got on either side of Grace. The little girl looked around with her big blue eyes for a moment, but they could see she was getting sleepy. Courtney tucked her blanket around her and buckled her own seat belt. She looked at Zoey and leaned over Grace to hug her.

"God heard us," Zoey whispered to Courtney. "I can't believe He answered our prayers!"

"Yes, He did," Courtney answered. "Believe it." Sitting back, they prepared for the long journey ahead. Courtney closed her eyes and gave a quick prayer of thanks to God. As she finished, she glanced out the window and saw a man entering the front door of the shelter. Her heart dropped as she noticed the man's familiar size and walk. It was Don!

Go, go, go! she thought as they left the parking lot. He had found her again. Fear prickled down her spine as she worried that even with the Scotts' assistance, she might never be rid of this horrid man.

Chapter 15

It took them several days to get home, and they were all tired when they finally arrived. They had gotten to know each other on the trip, and Courtney felt like one of the family. Zoey blossomed under her grandparents' care and concern, and she and Courtney grew even closer.

When they arrived, Courtney was blown away by their house in the hills of Kentucky. Her friend just smiled as she looked around.

"I forgot how beautiful it was," Zoey said to her grandparents.

"It really is," Courtney agreed. She saw the look of pride on their faces.

The house was a two-story, with lots of windows and soft-brown brick. There were tall white pillars in the front and a big sweeping porch across the back that overlooked rolling green hills for miles. Inside, everything was high ceilings and open space, with one room running right into the next. Upstairs there were two bedrooms at the front and a small sitting room and balcony overlooking the rooms below. The girls had the entire upstairs to themselves, since Grandma Mary (as she had insisted Courtney call her) had undergone knee surgery the year before and had moved into the master suite on the lower level.

The bedrooms each had their own bathrooms, with the open balcony and sitting room in the middle. Since one of the bedrooms had already been decorated for Zoey, Courtney would have the other side, which was done in light yellows, making it look like sunshine filled the room. There was a Queen-sized bed and matching dresser and nightstand and the floors were shiny hardwood that was obviously real wood. A huge rug in soft green and blue tones covered most of the floor that wasn't taken up by furniture. The room was spacious and airy, just like the rest of the house.

"There's a small crib and assorted baby items in the basement"—Grandma Mary showed Courtney the room—"and a big rocking chair. I'll have Tom carry the crib and chair upstairs for you. You and Zoey can look through the rest of it."

Courtney turned and hugged her without hesitation. She knew God had sent this wonderful woman to help her, and she was humbled by their continued care and generosity.

Grandma Mary left to check on Zoey, and Courtney just stood there looking around the room. After the shelter, this room looked amazing. Courtney had lived in a beautiful home with Don and her mother, but it had been Don's house first, and it lacked the warmth of the Scott home. Courtney saw the warm touches that Mary had added: the little lamp on the nightstand, the big clock on the wall, and two beautiful pictures of sunflowers.

Walking into the bathroom, she stopped in awe. Everything was so pretty! There was an old-fashioned white tub in one corner with a soft yellow towel and matching washcloth hanging over the side. A glassed-in shower took up most of the other side of the bathroom, except for a tiny little room that held the toilet, with a door to close it off from the rest of the room. The sink and vanity filled the other wall, with a large sink that Courtney was quite sure she could bathe the baby in. Everything was spotless! On the trip to Kentucky, Zoey had shared that Grandma Mary had a cleaning lady who came once a week. Grandpa Tom had insisted on it after her knee surgery. It was all so beautiful Courtney wanted to cry.

Speaking of crying, Courtney heard the baby crying softly in the next room. She hurried over to her and got her out of her new car seat. She walked her around the room, showing her everything. Then she put her in her baby sling, and they wandered over to Zoey's room to see how she was doing.

Zoey's room was done in pink and a beautiful peachy color. There was a comforter on her bed that picked up the colors in big bright poppies. Her rug was round and fluffy, with little bits of the same colors scattered throughout. There was a dressing table with a mirror, in addition to her dresser and nightstand. A huge brown bear was propped up in the corner, next to a tall narrow bookshelf that held books in all shapes and colors. Zoey was going through the closet in the room, holding up some of the clothes that were much too small for her now—cute little dresses and coats that would have fit a much smaller girl.

"Guess you've grown a little since your last visit, huh," Courtney said with a smile.

"I can't believe it has been so long since I visited," Zoey replied. "Grams and Pops kept begging us to come for a visit, and we were just so busy." Tears threatened as she continued, "I wish they had gotten to see my mom and dad one more time."

Courtney gathered Zoey to her and Grace, hugging her tightly. "I'm so sorry," she told Zoey. "So, so sorry. I know just how you feel. I would give anything to see my mom again . . . or to go back to how it was when Daddy was alive." The girls held each other with the infant between them. Their shared grief tightened their bond. Finally, Courtney broke away and put a smile on her face. "Grandma Mary said there were baby items in the basement. Do you want to help us find them? This little one could use a few things." She gave the infant a pat and tickled her little tummy.

"Of course I do," Zoey replied. "Let's go."

Downstairs, Grandma Mary was out of sight in her own room, putting away things from their trip. She came out to the living area when she heard the girls come down the stairs.

"I thought we might just warm up some soup tonight for supper," she told the girls. "I think we need today to get settled. Then tomorrow we can go to the grocery store and do a little shopping. I would love it if you girls would come along. We could stop at the mall beforehand, if you like. You girls can't live in those clothes you got from the shelter. You'll need some more things and some toiletries and such. It's been so long since I have been able to spoil this one." She gave her granddaughter a squeeze. "And now I have a couple more girls to spoil. It will be such fun!"

Before Courtney could say anything, she told the girls to go on down to the basement if they wanted to look at the baby things. She was going to take a shower, and then she would come out and see what they had found. She disappeared before either of the girls could say a word.

"Wow," Courtney said.

"I know," Zoey replied. "She's always like that. She just pushes everybody along with her. But she's really wonderful, Courtney. I hope you don't mind." She could see the worry in Courtney's eyes and didn't want her to think badly of Grams. She loved her so much. Courtney confirmed her fears with her next words.

"I just don't want her to think she has to buy things for me and the baby," she told Zoey. "We aren't her responsibility, and it'll be expensive for all three of us. Besides, I also don't want to take away from what she would do for you."

Zoey could tell her friend was nervous about it. "Courtney," she started, "first, my grandparents have more money than they'll ever spend. They were both attorneys and only had one child, my mom, so they have always been able to have the best. That's not to brag, just to tell you that Grams will love having three girls to dress up and buy things for. It's what she does! Please, don't take that away from her. This is going to be so much fun for her. She's always wanted more grandchildren, and now she has all of us. Besides, I think it will lessen her grief about losing my folks."

The girls headed down to the basement. They stopped and petted Max, the family dog. Grandpa Tom had picked him up while Grandma Mary was showing them their rooms. Then they followed Grandpa Tom down to the basement.

He had already carried the crib upstairs and was going back down to get the rocking chair. Zoey stopped and helped him get it up the two flights of stairs. While Courtney waited, she marveled at the neat rows of shelves and boxes and stuff. Zoey returned, and they wandered around looking for baby things, finally locating them in the back corner of the basement. A playpen was folded up against the wall, and a high chair and stroller leaned on the adjacent wall. There was also a baby swing high up on a shelf and a couple of plastic tubs that were labeled *Zoey's baby clothes*. There was a small step ladder that was obviously used to add and remove the plastic tubs and boxes when needed.

Zoey got the ladder and climbed up to get the baby swing and brought it down. They brushed it off and placed the little girl in it. The swing had a large white knob on one side, and when they wound it up, it played music. Grace's big blue eyes opened wide as she swung back and forth to the music. Before long, the swing lulled her fast asleep. The girls laughed, and Zoey went back up the ladder to get one of the tubs of baby clothes. After she handed it down to Courtney, they decided to carry things upstairs before going through them. Courtney picked up the sleeping Grace, carrying her swing and all, while Zoey carried the big plastic tub of clothes.

Once upstairs, they had fun sorting through the toys and clothing in the tub. Courtney was hesitant to take things for the baby, but Zoey was insistent. She held things up to Grace, trying to figure out what size she needed. The zero to three months seemed about right. She sorted out sleepers and outfits for the little girl, socks and bibs, and a big fuzzy peach blanket. They found sheets for the crib, some baby towels and washcloths, and a tiny pink comb and brush set. They put the rest of the clothing back in the tub to go back to the basement, and Zoey carried it down.

By the time Zoey got back upstairs, Grandma Mary had cleaned the crib, wiped down the mattress, and asked Grandpa Tom to take the crib upstairs to their room. She was taking the bedding to the washing machine, so she stopped and picked up the clothing and other items the girls had selected, then carried it all to the washer in a laundry room off the kitchen. Grace slept happily in the swing the whole time.

When the clothing and bedding were dry and folded, Courtney made a bottle and took the baby upstairs to feed her and change her before supper. Zoey followed her with the clean laundry, dropping it off before she went on to her own room. Grandpa Tom had put the rocker in the corner of their bedroom and placed the crib nearby. Once the baby was fed and dry, Courtney placed her back in her baby seat. She got one of the clean sheets for the crib and put it on the mattress so it would be all ready when it was time for bed.

Trying it out, she picked up the infant and laid her in the crib. Grandpa Tom had attached a small mobile of baby animals just above one end of the crib that wound up and played music. As the baby tried to focus on the little animals above her, Courtney wound the mobile and the music began. The fascinated baby watched the little animals go round and round to "Twinkle, Twinkle Little Star," and Courtney was sure she saw a smile on her tiny face. After a few minutes, she picked her up and headed down for supper.

Chapter 16

Supper was a happy affair, though simple, with hot soup and fresh muffins that Grandma Mary had baked while Courtney was feeding the baby. They placed the infant in the swing at the end of the table, where she was content to sit as they all ate supper. After supper the girls helped stack the dishes in the dishwasher and take care of the leftovers. Then they went outside to water Max and give him his supper. Max was a beautiful Australian Shepherd. He was old, but very friendly. Courtney thought he was perfect—a beautiful dog for a beautiful family.

They put an old movie on, content to just sit and enjoy being home. No more traveling for a while. Grandma Mary was happy to hold Grace, and the baby seemed content in her arms. Courtney could hear her cooing and calling the baby a pretty girl.

First thing the next day, Grandma Mary was ready to go to the mall and grocery store. Shopping with Zoey's grandma was a treat for the girls. They brought the stroller up from the basement and wiped the dust off. When they got to the mall, they placed the infant in the stroller and began walking around. Whenever Grandma Mary saw something in the window of a store that she thought the girls would like, she took the stroller and insisted the girls go in and check it out. Zoey found some cute jeans and a top, and Grandma Mary insisted Courtney do the same.

When they came out with their purchases, Grandma Mary was leaving Gymboree with some bags of her own. Grace sat in the stroller holding a brand-new toy in her little hand, but she was fast asleep. Burlington Coat Factory, Journeys, Garage, Victoria's Secret, and Macy's—they visited them all. At lunchtime they stopped at the food court to get some food. Courtney had packed a bottle of warm water and quickly made the baby a bottle. She was becoming a pro at making bottles. Grandma Mary and Zoey picked up some subs and drinks while Courtney sat and fed Grace. After they finished their lunch, they went to the women's room, where Courtney could change the baby.

When Courtney thanked Grandma Mary for the tenth time that day, Grandma Mary turned and wrapped her arms around the girl. She took Courtney's face in her hands and look at her with love and compassion.

"Look," she said to her, "I love my granddaughter and she loves you. It's obvious to me how much you and she have connected after all that you have both gone through the past few days. You have no one left to look after you, and I think your mother would want you to be part of a good family. We are good people, Courtney, and we're willing to love you and take care of you and Grace. Can you let that be enough, at least for now? Tom and I can help you with the rest of the details later. It's going to be okay." She dropped her hands and hugged Courtney again.

Courtney could do nothing but nod her head and hug her back.

After the mall they all went to the grocery store and picked up groceries. Grandma Mary encouraged the girls to add things they liked, and they planned some meals together. She took them to the baby section and asked them to pick out the things Grace needed. Zoey added diapers, soap, ointment, and baby Tylenol to the cart, while Courtney picked out more powdered formula and a pack of baby wipes.

When they returned home, Courtney took the infant upstairs to finish her nap. Placing her in the clean crib and turning on the little mobile made Courtney feel like a real mom. Tears rolled down her cheeks as she thought about her own mom, but she knew in her heart that her mom would have loved Grandma Mary and Grandpa Tom. She planned to ask them to help her find out what had happened to her mom for sure, then figure out how to get custody of Grace. Their background in law should make it easier.

"Thank you, God," Courtney said quietly. "Thank you for bringing these wonderful people into my life and giving me this beautiful little girl to take care of. I am so glad that you are back in my life and so thankful for your grace and understanding. Forgive me for the years I tried to push you out. And, God, please give my dad and mom a hug for me if they're with you. Amen."

After a few days, Courtney began to feel at ease staying with the Scotts. She felt pretty confident that Don didn't know her whereabouts, did not even know her name or that she had an infant with her. She hated that he wouldn't be made to pay for what he had done in Colorado, but at least he would never get the opportunity to hurt her or her mom.

One night, when Courtney got up in the night and had to go down to make the baby another bottle, Grandpa Tom was sitting in the living room watching television.

"Couldn't sleep," he said to Courtney as she started toward the kitchen to make a bottle. "Hand me Grace while you fix her a bottle."

Courtney placed the infant in his arms and walked over to the kitchen. She could still see Grandpa Tom and the baby as she got out the formula. He was such a cute grandpa, and Courtney felt so happy to see him cooing at the baby and laughing at the faces she made in return. It was all so natural and loving. She walked back to the living area to take the baby, but Grandpa Tom took the bottle instead.

"Sit down and take a load off," he told Courtney. She sat across from them as he fed the little girl. After a few minutes, he looked over and smiled at Courtney. "She sure is a cute little thing. You're a great mom, Courtney. You know that, right?"

Courtney was a bit uncomfortable when he put it that way, and she was afraid Grandpa Tom could sense her unease. "I . . . um . . . yeah, I guess so." She was shaky and knew he picked up on it.

"What's the matter, honey?" he said quietly. "Is there something you aren't telling us? You can trust us, you know. We only have your best interests at heart, and we love having you and this little sweetie with us. We'll do everything in our power to protect you and her, just as if you were our own."

Courtney didn't know if it was because she was tired, because Grandpa Tom was so sweet, or just because she didn't like hiding anything from these nice people, but suddenly she just wanted to get it all out in the open. "She isn't mine, Grandpa Tom. I found her floating in the river after the hurricane, and I rescued her."

At Tom's look of surprise, she found herself needing to go on. "I was in this boat, and she just came floating along in her baby seat, and I grabbed her. When we ran the boat into this church and I took her out of her baby seat, there was this note. It was from her mom. It said she couldn't go on and asked whoever found her to take care of her, tell her she was sorry. I had to keep her!"

Courtney was almost sobbing, but she went on. "Then we got rescued and everyone thought she was mine, so I didn't say anything. I think her mother is gone, and she said there was no one to help her. I kept checking the notes at the shelters that people left if they were looking for someone, but here was no one looking for a baby girl. Then we moved to the other shelter after I thought my stepfather was following me. He's not a nice man, Grandpa Tom, and he knows I discovered something about his past. I'm afraid of him. Then we met Zoey, and she looked so sad, but she helped me with the baby, and we both felt an instant bond. So much happened so fast I couldn't keep up with it all, but Grace needs me. I worry that someone will take her from me. I have prayed about all of it, every night, and I think God wants me to take care of her."

Suddenly she just stopped talking. She had gone on and on and on. She realized how much she had told Grandpa Tom, and she felt sick to her stomach. What would he think?

Grandpa Tom just looked at Courtney. The baby had finished her bottle and fallen back asleep, so he got up and laid her on the couch, putting a pillow in front of her. He walked over and sat down on the oversized hassock that matched the chair Courtney was sitting in, noticing that she had a look of utter despair on her face.

"Oh, you poor girl," Grandpa Tom said. "You've been carrying the weight of the world on your young shoulders, haven't you?" He put his big arms around Courtney and hugged her. "It's going to be okay, honey. I promise you we will do everything we can to help you."

Courtney couldn't help herself. All this time she had held in her grief for her mother and her worry and fear about Don, and she just couldn't anymore. She sobbed out her grief and worry and fear. And Grandpa Tom cried a few tears of his own as he held her.

Once her tears ran dry, Grandpa Tom handed Courtney a box of tissues and took one himself. She saw the understanding and compassion on his face, and for the first time since the storm, she felt like she had somebody on her side. So she finished her story. She told Grandpa Tom about the night of the storm and watching her mom be swept away. She told him about her battle with her faith after her father had died and how the storm and the church and the baby had brought her back to believing. And of course God had been there too, through all of it.

Grandpa Tom just listened and held her hand and nodded once in a while. When she was finally exhausted, he talked to her quietly.

"You're right to turn back to God and believe in Jesus Christ as your Savior. Mary and I believe as well. You are a very brave young lady, and you've gone through an ordeal that most grown-ups wouldn't survive. You're safe with us, child, and I hope that this Don character is long gone. He better stay away from here, if he knows what's good for him!"

Courtney finally said good night, so thankful for this wonderful man. She picked up Grace and headed upstairs, where she laid the precious little baby girl in her bed and climbed into her own. She was exhausted, but she took a moment to thank God one more time, for His love and grace and guidance. It had brought her here to these wonderful people. Her last thought before falling sound asleep was, *I love you, Mom. I'll be okay.*

When Don walked inside the shelter in Tennessee, he quickly figured out who "Star" was. He had picked up a copy of the rescued list in Georgia and compared it to the one from the shelter in Tennessee, noting the name "Star Johnson" and infant daughter. That had to be Courtney. He had no idea who the infant was, but she must know he'd survived and was trying to get away. He would wait patiently for a couple of days. Once he was sure she wasn't here, he would follow Courtney, or Star as she was calling herself, to the shelter in Kentucky. She had nowhere else to go, with no means to support herself. She had to go to the shelter. He was done pretending to be her caring stepfather, and he was angry that she had resisted and eluded him.

Her running was almost over. He knew she knew about his past. He had taken her laptop and checked it himself. He had to stop her from telling anyone, just as he had stopped her mother, and the mother and daughter before them. The storm had made it easy with Courtney's mom. He had hoped to have both of them out there with him when it hit, knowing he had an inflatable life vest on under his sweatshirt and they did not. But the girl was frightened and wouldn't come out on the pier with them. And against all odds she had survived the hurricane. Bad luck for him, but he wasn't going to let some stupid girl bring the authorities back on his trail. He would find her and put an end to it. And he would have some fun scaring her first. He couldn't wait to see that terrified look on her face and let her know that he was the one in control, the one calling the shots now. He relished that. And her mom wasn't around to help her now. He had enjoyed a lifetime of using vulnerable women, then collecting tidy sums of money when they had "accidents." Once he took care of Courtney and cashed in on the insurance money, he was going to take a nice long vacation in Mexico before he looked for his next victim.

Chapter 17

Courtney called the shelters in Georgia and Tennessee daily, asking about Carol Dixson, her mom, hoping every time that her mom had finally made it to a shelter. She had decided she would give it at least a week before giving up. The Scotts had a memorial planned for Zoey's parents at the end of the week, and they had offered to do something similar for Courtney's mom. She just wasn't ready.

Grandma Mary looked up from the recipe she was reading as Courtney came into the kitchen and asked to use her phone, promising she would keep it short. She had offered to get the girls cell phones and had one ordered for Zoey, but Courtney wanted to wait until she could pay for her own. She was trying to find a job at a daycare center, where she could take Grace with her when she worked. She had already called on one that was hiring and she had aninterview later that week.

She dialed the number for the shelter in Georgia. The lady who answered was familiar with Courtney from the day before. As soon as Courtney gave her name, the tone of the lady's voice changed.

"I am so sorry, honey," she started.

"What do you mean?"

Grandma Mary looked up from her recipe at the tone of concern in Courtney's voice.

"We have started a list of people who did not survive the hurricane. Carol Dixson was added to that list last night. She had on a shirt from the office where she worked, and we were able to have a coworker identify her. I don't know what to say. I'm so sorry. We are trying to reach her husband, who was here a few days ago, but he didn't leave a number or address where he can be reached. Do you know how to contact him?"

Grandma Mary stood up and put her arms around Courtney, taking the phone as it fell from her lifeless fingers. She had heard everything and saw that Courtney was about to collapse.

"Thank you. We'll have to call you back." She put the phone down and helped the sobbing girl to a chair at the table, keeping her arm around her and pulling up another chair close to hers.

"Oh honey, I am so sorry!" She let Courtney cry until all her tears were spent.

"I-I knew she was probably gone," Courtney stammered. "Now it's for sure. I'll never see her again, Grandma Mary." Fresh tears rolled down her cheeks.

"Is there anyone else we should notify?" She handed her tissues from a box on the table.

"No," Courtney answered. "My mom's parents died in an auto accident and my dad's parents were already gone when I came along. It's just me and Don, her husband. He was with her when the storm hit, and I saw them get swept off the pier. I wonder if he even tried to help her, and I'm certainly not going to try to reach him!"

"You'll never know, but it's done, so you'll have to let it go. It's not for us to judge others, Courtney, hard as that may be at times. Do you want to try to go back there?"

"No! I couldn't bear seeing her like that. I just couldn't. Please." Courtney held on to Grandma Mary for dear life.

Grandma Mary patted her back, waiting for her to gain control. After a few minutes, she handed her a couple more tissues and shared a thought. "What if we just add a small memorial plate next to the one we are placing for Zoey's parents?"

Courtney looked up at her tearfully.

"You could put her name and dates on it and something to remember her by. Then you would have a place to visit when you want to talk to her. I know that's going to help us. Would you be interested in something like that?"

Courtney was starting to come to grips with the news. She thought about what Grandma Mary said for a minute, then nodded tearfully. "I think so," she said quietly. "I need to get Grace." She left the room in a hurry, and Grandma Mary let her go. She couldn't think straight right now. All she wanted was to get back to Grace and escape to her room.

Zoey was upstairs watching the baby, and when she got to her room, Grace was lying on a blanket playing with a small toy. Courtney scooped her up and hurried to her own room, leaving Zoey with a mumbled thank you.

Later that week, both girls attended the memorial service for their parents. Grandma Mary asked a neighbor to look after Grace, knowing it would be difficult for all of them. After the service they went to the cemetery, where two plates were placed side by side—one for Zoey's parents and one for Courtney's mom, with personalized messages on each. It was difficult to say their final goodbyes, but they had each other, and somehow that made it easier. Both girls were comforted by the thought that there were three new angels up in heaven watching over them.

Chapter 18

Courtney knew it was getting close to Christmas, but she was not excited. It was hard to imagine the holidays without her mom, even though she had wonderful "grandparents" like the Scotts. She and Zoey had talked, and agreed they both had a lot to be thankful for. It was so much easier to go on in a household where they could be together. They were convinced the friendship they had formed at the shelter would last a lifetime. Still, it was difficult to think about. They had made small gifts for the Scotts and Grace, but Courtney knew it was going to be an emotional holiday.

Since both of Courtney's parents were gone, the Scotts were petitioning the state of Florida to adopt her and Grace. Mary seemed pretty certain that eventually she and Tom could make it happen. It would be a long process, but they had reached out to a judge in Florida who was a longtime friend.

"I'm pretty optimistic about making it happen," Mary told Courtney. "Besides, with all of the claims and impacts on the system from the hurricane, by the time it gets around to our case, you might already be eighteen."

In the meantime, they were going to fill out the initial paperwork required as foster parents and turn it into the shelter here in Kentucky. The shelter had agreed to start the process, then send it on to Florida.

Courtney had already applied online for a new birth certificate so she could replace her driver's license. Her friend Maddison, back in Florida, tried to help from afar by sending some pictures of Courtney from their yearbook that showed her face and name, along with a library card of Courtney's she had borrowed. Courtney included them in her application, in an effort to provide additional proof of her identity. Everything had been lost in the hurricane, so she had to go through all the processes and paperwork to get it back. It all took so much time.

One afternoon, Grandma Mary mentioned that she had gotten a letter from the shelter in Tennessee reminding her about some information she had promised to give them when she picked up the girls. They also had an additional form that Courtney needed to sign saying she agreed to living with the Scotts. They could stop in at the shelter in Kentucky to drop of the paperwork and sign the additional document, and they would forward it to Tennessee for them.

Taking the paperwork to the Kentucky shelter frightened Courtney a little, but she wanted to be done with it. Grandma Mary had a doctor appointment the following day, which was just a couple of buildings away from the shelter. She suggested the girls go with her. They could walk over, sign the form, and drop off the paperwork at the shelter while Grams was at the doctor.

The next day was bright and sunny as they set out for the appointment. Once they arrived at the doctor's office, they split up. At the last minute, Zoey decided to stay with her grandma, so Courtney put the baby in her baby sling and took the papers. The sunshine lifted her spirits, even though it was cold. She was glad they had warm clothes on, even for the short walk.

Courtney put the fuzzy peach blanket over the little one in the sling, and away they went. They found the shelter easily and Courtney took the papers to one of the ladies up front. They gave her the form she needed, which she filled out and signed. As she was turning to head back, she ran in to Shannon Smith, the woman who had been on the boat with Courtney in Georgia when she was rescued.

The woman hugged Courtney and told her they were just about to leave, heading to Ohio to stay with some relatives there. She explained they had eventually wound up in the Kentucky shelter after more and more people were rescued and the shelters filled up. With Shannon having relatives in Ohio, the Kentucky shelter made sense for them because it was closer to where they were eventually heading. Shannon invited her back to say hello to her husband and daughter.

Once Courtney said her goodbyes to the Smiths, she was anxious to get back to Grandma Mary and Zoey. As she headed toward the front doors, she almost fainted when she saw Don coming in from the parking lot. He must still be looking for her at the shelters! Courtney turned around and raced back to where the Smiths were loading their car up at the back door to leave. All that mattered was getting away from Don.

"Hey, I've decided to go on to Ohio. Do you have room for us?" Courtney asked.

"Of course we do," Shannon replied. "Let me go back in and get you a car seat for the baby."

Desperate to get away before Don spotted her, Courtney waited in agony for Shannon to return. Finally, Shannon came out of the door smiling and carrying the seat that she told Courtney she could leave at the next shelter. They hooked it into the middle of the back seat and buckled Grace in, then were on their way to Ohio.

If she was lucky, Don would not even know they had been there. Maybe he would finally give up. There was no way she wanted him to find out she had been staying with the Scotts or figure out her connection to them and Zoey. She knew he would try to cause them harm if he suspected she had told them about his past. Once they got to Ohio, she would call her sweet adopted family and tell them not to worry. She checked the diaper bag to make sure she had the phone number and twenty-dollar bill that Grandma Mary had tucked in for emergencies. It took everything Courtney had to hold back the tears.

When they finally got to Ohio, Courtney thanked the Smiths and asked them to drop her at the shelter. She said goodbye, unbuckled the baby seat, and walked into the shelter. It was even colder in Ohio, and Courtney was glad she had on a coat and warm clothes. In the ladies' room, she changed Grace's diaper and tried to calm down.

"What have I done?"

She didn't realize she had said the words out loud until Grace squirmed in the sling, startled at the sound of her voice. After comforting her, she pulled out Grandma Mary's cell phone number and went to the front of the shelter to call. She remembered to take the baby out of the car seat and return it, placing her back in the sling. Then she asked if she could use the phone and walked across the room for privacy. She would try to keep it light, but she knew telling them she had left would be difficult. She dialed the number, and when they didn't answer, she left a message.

"Hey guys." Courtney tried to sound cheerful. "It's me! Listen, I met some friends when I stopped at the shelter, and they invited me to go to Ohio with them. I decided to go, and here I am. Sorry I didn't talk to you first, but don't worry about us. I'll be in touch soon. Thanks for everything!"

She hung up and handed the phone to the lady, then asked for it back and redialed, knowing it would go to voicemail.

"I saw Don at the shelter, and I was so scared! I asked the Smiths if I could ride with them to Ohio. I don't want him to know about you, because I'm afraid one of you could get hurt. I'll call you as soon as I can. Please understand. I'm so sorry!" She walked back to the desk and returned the phone, feeling only slightly better about being honest. Then she headed toward the back of the shelter before anyone could ask questions.

Passing the ladies' room again, Courtney went back inside. Thankfully, there was no one else in the room. She held Grace tightly as she leaned on the counter, sobbing. She thought about everything Zoey and the Scotts meant to her. She was miles and miles away from them, and she felt like she couldn't go on. She knew they would worry, in spite of her message.

And how could they ever forgive her? Why should they? And how was she going to take care of Grace? She could already tell this shelter wasn't as nice as the others; it wasn't as clean, and the walls were scuffed and had cracks.

But she was stuck here. She couldn't even ask for a room because her name would get added to the list out front. She could use another name, but she didn't want to chance it anymore. Don must know she was using the name "Star," and now she knew he was still looking for her. He probably even knew she was traveling with a baby.

She fingered the locket around her neck with tears running down her cheeks. She had faced losing her mom, and now Zoey and the Scotts were lost as well. She hugged Grace tightly to her body, seeing the bright-blue eyes looking up at her, trusting *her*. She had to be strong for Grace.

Chapter 19

Courtney finally left the restroom and walked to the back of the shelter. She saw several empty rooms and decided to go into one until someone told her she couldn't. She went into the first empty room she came to that had two cots in it and closed the little makeshift door.

What was she going to do?

Tears still poured down her face. Thankfully, the little one was finally sleeping. She knew she had upset Grace, and she was sorry the baby had to be part of the mess she had made of things.

"Dear God," she prayed, "please help me. This little one needs us both now, and I really don't know what to do. I have lost everything again, and I don't think I can handle it. I can't even count on this shelter, because I know Don will come and find me. Please send someone to help us. Amen."

While Courtney worried about her own situation, another young runaway sat in the room next to hers. Jeremiah Stewart was at his wits' end himself and was trying to decide what his next move was going to be. He had saved a little money from odd jobs and by eating at the shelter whenever he could. He needed a hot shower and food.

He heard Courtney crying in the room next door and was momentarily distracted from his own problems. He knocked on her door.

"One minute," Courtney said as she heard the knock. Thinking she was going to have to leave, she gathered up the baby and her small diaper bag as she opened the door.

"I was just leaving," she started, surprised when she saw a disheveled guy standing there.

"Are you okay?" he asked her.

"I'm fine," Courtney replied. "I'm just leaving." She tried to brush by him with the baby.

"Wait," he said. "I came to help. You look like you could use a friend."

"Why do you even care?" Courtney asked him, irritated that he was bothering her. Then she remembered her prayer.

"Well, you have a baby, and you seem upset. Do you want to get a bite to eat? I have a little money, and you might feel better. My name is Miah, by the way."

At that moment Courtney just wanted out of the shelter. Don could have followed them here; he could be walking in any minute. She didn't want to be anywhere near it, since that seemed to be the way he was tracking her. Maybe this guy knew another place she could stay.

Maybe God had sent him to help. He certainly looked harmless . . . and tired.

"Sure," Courtney replied. "Do you know a quiet place nearby . . . a public place?" She wanted to let him know that she did not trust him completely.

"Yes," Miah said. "It's a couple of streets over, but it's clean and quiet and cheap. Do you mind the walk?"

"No. Let's just go, okay?"

She still felt desperate and upset, and she couldn't hide the fact that she wanted to leave the shelter as soon as possible. If this guy, Miah, could help, she was all for it. She followed him out the back door of the building, feeling like she had no other choice at the moment.

Once they arrived at the café, Miah led her to a quiet booth in the back corner of the restaurant where she could see the door but was somewhat protected from sight by the partition between booths.

"They always have a four-dollar special here," he said shyly. "Today it looks like grilled cheese and tomato soup. Are you okay with that?" When she nodded, he ordered it for both of them. The waitress put in their order and brought them ice water. There was an awkward silence between them, so Miah made an attempt at conversation.

"What's your name?" he asked quietly.

Courtney looked at him with her troubled eyes and remembered to use her fake name. "It's Star," she said nervously.

"And the baby," Miah continued, "is it a girl or boy?"

"Girl." Tears welled up in Courtney's eyes. "She's all I have."

"Well, let's not worry about that right now," Miah said. "I'm on the run from an abusive foster care situation. It doesn't get much worse than that, right? I have no home and no job, unless I can find someone willing to pay me to do some menial task. And I have nothing but a backpack of a few essentials to call my own. But we have to eat, and we have to believe there's something better in the future."

For the first time since they had met, Courtney noticed this boy. How old could he be . . . maybe sixteen or seventeen? He wasn't any older than she was, and here she was focusing on only her problems. What had he gone through? What was his story? Knowing there was nothing but uncertainty ahead of her, Courtney decided to think of someone other than herself for a change and let this boy and his circumstances distract her from her own dilemma.

After a few moments of silence, during which she automatically patted the little bundle in her arms, she looked at Miah.

"Miah, right?" she asked him. "Why are you all alone?"

"My mom died when I was ten, and I went into the foster system. Nobody wanted a kid my age, so they kept moving me around for years. About two years ago, I was sent to a home where they starved me and beat me. I couldn't take it, so I ran."

Courtney couldn't believe he had actually been on the run for two years. He had made it this long on his own. Could she do that?

Their soup and sandwiches had come and gone while Miah told his story, but incredibly he still managed to make her feel like he cared about her in spite of his own situation. In fact, just like with Zoey, in some way it actually connected them. As Miah finished, telling her he was talking far too much, he gave her a tiny bit of something that she really needed.

"I still remember my mom," he said, "She's what keeps me going. I try to go to church when I can and remember what she always told me as a child: 'God is with you, and there is always hope.' Do you believe in God, Star?"

She didn't respond for a moment. This was the second time someone was asking her if she believed in God. Was He reminding her?

"Did I get your name wrong? It's Star, right?"

"Yes, of course," she finally answered.

The baby started to fuss a little, and Courtney excused herself to go to the restroom and change her. She asked Miah to get a glass of warm water so she could make her a bottle. When she returned with the dry baby, she pulled out the bottle she had packed with formula already measured inside and poured in the warm water that had been delivered while she was gone. Shaking the bottle expertly, she smiled at Miah. She pulled the baby up a bit in the sling, holding the bottle against her chest so the hungry little girl could eat.

"Sorry. Yes, Miah," she finally answered. "I do believe in God."

Courtney went on to tell him her story. She told him about the hurricane in Florida and her trips to the different shelters. She told him about Zoey and living with the Scotts. Finally, she told him about Don and his reasons for wanting to find her, maybe even wanting to kill her. It was starting to get dark by the time she finished, and she could tell the café was ready to close. The waitress kept looking at them and was putting stuff away.

"I think we better go." Courtney gathered the empty bottle and stood up with the now-sleeping baby. "The waitress is putting things away and filling the salt and pepper shakers, so I think she wants to close. I guess I'll have to go back to the shelter. I have a little money, so I can pay."

"I already took care of the food while you were in the restroom," Miah answered. "Do you really think Don followed you here?"

"I don't know for sure. I don't think he had time to actually follow the car that the Smiths were driving, but he will probably ask questions and find out that I left with them. It's only a matter of time before he gets to Ohio, and I'm pretty sure he'll go to the shelter to see if we're there. That's why I didn't sign us in or ask for anything. I don't even want the shelter knowing I'm here."

"Well, I know another place you can stay," Miah said. "But it's a little rough, and there's nothing there besides what we take. Do you have more diapers and formula for the baby?"

"No," Courtney said. "I thought we were only going to be gone for a couple of hours. Maybe I could go back to the shelter and get some formula and diapers. All I have is one more diaper and the bottle of water I didn't use for the baby. Why were you at the shelter today? I thought you must be staying there."

"I do stay there sometimes," he told her, "when I need some food or a hot shower. But I try not to stay in one place too long because I don't want people noticing and asking me questions. I'm afraid they'll take me back, and I couldn't bear that. I just slip into one of the empty rooms in the back when I need to shower or eat, and nobody even notices. The shelter is never full, and as long as you don't stay too long, they don't notice. Hold on."

Miah got up and went over to the girl who had waited on them. It was pretty obvious that she was preparing the café for closing, pulling down the blinds and emptying trash cans, but she smiled and nodded at something Miah told her. He walked back to their table.

"Lizzy is going to let you stay here while I run back to the shelter and see what I can find. She'll put the *Closed* sign out, but she knows me and will let you stay while she finishes cleaning up. I can hurry. Are you okay staying here for a few minutes?"

Courtney nodded and looked over at Lizzy, who smiled at her. Then she looked back at Miah, thankful he was here and willing to help. She pulled the last diaper out of the bag and gave it to him so he would know the size and told him to look for formula in a canister that was for babies from birth to six months.

He raced off, as if on a mission.

Lizzy walked over and admired the little girl. "I have to go in the back to put things away for the night."

Courtney smiled and looked around after she had gone, feeling strange and a little frightened now that Miah wasn't there

After about fifteen minutes, she saw Miah return, rattling the back door, which Lizzy had already locked. She opened it and let Miah in. Courtney already had her coat in hand, so she picked up her bag and followed Miah out the door he had just entered.

Chapter 20

Courtney was nervous, but she could tell they were headed back toward the shelter. If she didn't like what Miah had in mind, she could always go back there and take her chances with running into Don. About halfway between the café and the shelter, they turned the corner, and she spotted a small white church up ahead. Across the street was another white building with a *Welcome!* sign across the door. Miah headed toward the second building.

As they got closer, Courtney could see it was weathered building that needed a coat of paint. Miah opened the door and they stepped inside. There was an old leather sofa on one side of the room, with a pillow and a couple of blankets, and another old stuffed sofa against the other wall. The room was warm but smelled a little like stale crackers and bleach.

As they stood just inside the door, an elderly man came into the room from a long hallway. He was eating a sandwich. "Hey, Miah," he said with a toothless grin. "Cold out there tonight. Who's this?"

"This is Courtney and her baby," Miah answered, assuming like everyone else that the baby was hers. "Is the loft empty tonight?"

"Sure is," the old man replied. "Martha just washed the sheets and made up the bed this afternoon."

"Okay if she uses it tonight?" Miah asked. He didn't offer any more information.

The old man reached up to a ring holder on the wall and pulled off a key. "Surprised you don't want it yourself young man," he sputtered. "But sure, she can use it. Just let me know when she is leaving so we can clean it up. Appreciate your help with that, as usual!"

"Thanks, Fred." Miah shook the man's wrinkled hand and led Courtney around the corner to a door that he unlocked with the key. The door opened to a set of stairs that led up to the room he called the loft. When they reached the top the name of the room made more sense. It was slanted with a large opening that took up most of one wall and overlooked the room below. There was a bed and nightstand against the other wall, with a faded quilt hanging over the arm of a small rocking chair. The bed was covered in another quilt and had a flat pillow at the top and a neatly folded blanket across the end.

"I know it isn't much," Miah told her, "but it's quiet and clean and beats running into Don at the shelter. I help out here sometimes, stay up here whenever I can. There's a big room downstairs that has rows of beds, but I thought you would like this for the baby. It's much quieter up here. I can crash down there on the sofa where we came in." He pointed through the opening in the wall where she could look down and see the couch with the pillow and blankets they had seen when they came in.

"Its fine," Courtney said quietly. "I'm really tired, and it'll be a relief not to have to watch for Don."

"There are restrooms just down the hall at the bottom of the stairs. I can show you and then you can get some sleep." Miah led Courtney back down the stairs, where he pointed out the direction of the restrooms. "Do you need anything else?"

"Nope. I have the formula and diapers you got from the shelter and water to make a bottle. It's been a very long day. I'm ready to crash." She headed down to use the restroom, then came back and made her way upstairs with Grace. She had washed her face and hands and wanted nothing more than to feed Grace and go to sleep.

She sat in the rocker and fed the baby and had just changed her diaper when Miah knocked at the bottom of the stairs and came up carrying a cradle. It had a thick pad in the bottom and swung between two sturdy posts. Miah set it next to the small bed and took the quilt off the rocking chair to lay it in the bottom. Courtney placed the baby in it, and she was almost instantly asleep. It was perfect.

Miah smiled and said good night and made his way back down to the couch, where he prepared a spot for himself.

Courtney pulled down the quilt on the bed and spread the blanket across the top. She took off her coat and shoes and crawled under the covers. The long, emotional day had taken its toll, and she was asleep before she had time to think about it.

Courtney woke up the next morning to find Grace looking at her through the slats in the side of the cradle. Startled, she sat up, trying to get her bearings.

After feeding the baby and changing her diaper, Courtney put her back in the cradle, made the bed, and folded up the blankets. Picking up Grace, she put her in her sling and went down to the restroom. There she found packaged toothbrushes and toothpaste tubes in a big jar that said *Help yourself.* Grateful, she took one of the packets and brushed her teeth, then went looking for Miah.

He was just coming in the door when she got downstairs.

"I just came from the shelter and Don's name is not on the list there," he said. "I looked around and didn't see anyone that looked the way you described him, so I took a quick shower." His hair was still wet. "They're getting ready to serve breakfast," he continued. "Do you want to get something to eat? It's bright and sunny outside, and we could go for a walk afterward if you like."

Courtney could not resist Miah's attempt to help her and his desire to spend time with them. He had shared the night before that he was very lonely, although happy to be out of the abusive foster situation. She couldn't imagine having only yourself to rely on, no one to share things with. Miah was a pleasure to be with, thoughtful and caring. It would be nice to have someone to spend time with after breakfast—since Zoey and the Scotts were so far away—out of view of the shelter where Don would be looking for her. Besides, she was hungry.

"Okay," she told Miah. "I just have to keep an eye out for Don while we're at the shelter."

"We'll make it quick and get out of there," he told Courtney. "Then we can go for a nice walk far away from the shelter. There is a wooded area just outside of town with a path where we can walk, and no one will see us. I will help you keep a look out for Don."

As they walked over to the shelter, Miah told Courtney about the outreach center they had stayed in the night before. "You can almost always find a place to sleep there," he said. "And Fred is harmless, although he likes to talk. He lets me help tidy up around the place and keeps his ears open for odd jobs that people need help with. He saves the loft for me whenever he can. His wife, Martha, helps the staff with housecleaning. The church across the street actually maintains the center, but Fred and Martha are retired and live there, making sure people have what they need. Once a month all the teens from the church come over and give it a thorough cleaning. But they don't serve meals, except on special occasions, and they don't have showers. So I still have to go to the shelter pretty regularly."

Courtney smiled at Miah's chatter, patting Grace as they walked along. When they got to the shelter, they had a quick breakfast of eggs with bacon, toast, and juice, then were on their way without any trouble. They grabbed four bottles of water, which they put in Courtney's bag. She had rinsed Grace's bottle and put formula powder in it so she could add water to make a fresh bottle for the infant.

Forty-five minutes later, they reached the edge of the forest that Miah had mentioned. It was quite a hike for Courtney, especially carrying the infant in her sling. She could tell that Miah was already fit from all of the walking he did, but he was a good sport about going slow enough for her to keep up. They finally sat down on a bench at the edge of the forest, glad they had thought to bring the water. After Courtney had gotten back to normal breathing, they headed down the path that Miah had mentioned.

The path took them into the woods, and the two talked easily. They had overcome their initial shyness and felt more and more relaxed with each other. At one point, Courtney stopped to change Grace at a convenient spot where there was a rough bench and a trash can. The baby was smiling and cooing now, and Miah spoke to her easily, having spent a lot of time with other children at foster homes. But she still hadn't shared the baby's name or how she had rescued her.

Courtney was able to open up to Miah in more detail about what she had gone through with the loss of her father and now her mother. She could understand and share in Miah's feeling of being all alone in the world.

She told him again about meeting Zoey and how much she missed her and the Scotts. She just had to make sure that Don wasn't following her before she could take a chance and go back to Kentucky. Still, she didn't tell him her real name either.

Courtney didn't realize how far they had gone until they heard something in the distance and the path opened up abruptly to a beautiful sight. A small waterfall fell down from a high cliff—a long, sharp drop down to what appeared to be a large river that flowed through the forest. They could see what looked like a small deserted area of beach around the bend in the river.

"It's so beautiful," Courtney exclaimed in awe, getting a bit too close to the edge until Miah pulled her back to the path. "What fun it would be to find that little beach at the bottom and come here when it's warmer and we could put our feet in!"

"Maybe in the spring or summer," he agreed, "if you're still around."

Courtney looked at him questioningly but let it go.

"I think there should be a gate or something across the path to keep people from falling," Miah added. They turned around and headed back the way they had come.

Chapter 21

The next day, Miah suggested they go to the church for the sunrise breakfast they had every Sunday. Then they could attend the service afterward. Courtney looked down at her clothes and was thankful that the jeans and sweater did not look too bad after sleeping in them. Still, she questioned whether she was properly dressed for church.

"Star," Miah said to her wisely, "God doesn't care how you look, right? You told me His love was unconditional and available to everyone."

Smiling, she looked back at this young man who was so much wiser than he realized. "You're right," she told Miah. "God is with us, and there is always hope." She smiled, seeing a look on Miah's face that told her how much it meant to him to hear those words that his mother had repeated so many times during his early childhood.

The church was small and comfortable, and the people made them feel welcome. They took a seat on one of the pews at the back of the church. The music was soothing, and the pastor's message was about perseverance. He talked about making the right choices and not giving up when things got tough.

Miah leaned over to Courtney and whispered in her ear, "I think this message was written for us." They smiled at each other.

At the end of the service, the pastor read Romans 15:13: "Now may the God of hope fill you with all joy and peace in believing, that you may abound in hope by the power of the Holy Spirit." Miah reached over and squeezed Courtney's hand, and once again she was reminded that God was with her.

After that day, Miah and Courtney fell into a kind of pattern. They would spend a couple of days at the outreach center, where Fred left the cradle in the loft for the baby, since most people weren't aware that the loft existed. Miah would sleep downstairs on the couch, or in the room down the hall where they had rows of beds in one room for men and another for women. They went to the shelter for hot meals and showers, with Miah always checking first to make sure Don's name hadn't been added to the list and there was no one that fit his description lurking around. Sometimes they found extra rooms where they could spend the night, but Courtney preferred her little loft at the outreach center. They picked up some extra clothes for Courtney and the baby and found a large box to store them in.

Courtney had come to trust Miah after seeing how carefully he looked for Don at the shelter and made sure they had what they needed. She caught him looking at her and Grace with longing sometimes, and she knew he was starting to care for her and the baby. She still missed Zoey and the Scotts, though, so went to the front desk and she called Zoey's grandmother again when they were at the shelter and Miah was showering.

"I miss you all so much," she almost sobbed to Zoey, thankful her friend answered. "But I have to make sure Don hasn't followed me here. I won't take a chance of him connecting me to your family. He is bad news, Zoey!"

"Please, just let us come and get you," Zoey begged her.

"I can't. I'm not letting him get to any of you through me." She tried to distract Zoey by telling her about the beautiful waterfall she and Miah had discovered in the forest, but the line went quiet, and she didn't think Zoey was listening. "I have to go. Tell Grandma Mary and Grandpa Tom we're fine and I'll call again soon. I love you, Zoey!"

She hung up and handed the phone back before she could beg them to come get her. She was starting to wonder if she would ever get back to them. It seemed like a lifetime ago. She really wanted to go back to Kentucky. She was thinking about asking Miah to go too. He had found a job doing some work in an old building, hauling trash out to a big industrial dumpster. It didn't pay a lot, but, like Miah said, something was better than nothing. Still, it was warmer in Kentucky, and she was sure he could find a job there as well.

Christmas came and went, and Courtney and Miah agreed that presents were something they couldn't afford, and Grace wouldn't understand the significance of the day at her young age anyway. Still, Courtney found a cute teddy bear at the shelter for the baby, tucking it in beside her with a kiss on Christmas Eve.

Miah continued to work at the old building site, thankful that his assistance was still needed on the project. New Year's Day brought little change to their routine, but that night they celebrated the new year by having supper at a local burger joint. It felt good to do something together that they had actually earned themselves, or at least Miah had. They had already used the "emergency" money that Grandma Mary had given Courtney to buy formula when they couldn't find more at the shelter. It was just small packets of formula this time, and they hoped that the shelter would have another canister soon. Grace was consuming more and more formula every day, which was a concern to Courtney. She checked the shelter every time they went there in hopes of stockpiling a little extra, but lately they had not been carrying as much. They splurged and had sundaes for desert, although Courtney fretted about spending the extra money.

"Stop worrying," Miah told her. "I'll get more tomorrow."

Looking down at the infant sleeping innocently in her baby sling, Courtney thought she would never stop worrying. "Promise me you'll take care of her or find her a good home if anything happens to me," she said out of the blue.

"Nothing is going to happen to you. Don't say that," Miah answered with a smile.

Courtney looked at him solemnly.

"Okay, okay," he added. "I promise."

That night, Courtney tried to recall the verse she and Zoey had remembered from their Bible study and used as part of their prayer. Something about not being anxious and bringing your difficult situations to God. When she and Miah had gone to church on Sunday, Courtney had kept the little black Bible that was available for anyone to take home. She had started praying every night again. She kept the tiny Bible under her pillow, and it gave her strength. She tried to share her worries with God. She wanted him to know she believed in Him.

They were back at the outreach center that night, planning to check out the shelter the next day so they could get hot food and showers. Peeking through the opening in the loft, Courtney could see that Miah was already asleep, exhausted after a full day of hauling trash. Grace was sleeping as well, so she pulled out her little Bible, straining to read in the dim light. The Bible opened to the book of Psalms, and Courtney strained to read some of the verses. Suddenly she found what she was looking for—Psalm 118:14. It was so simple: "The Lord is my strength and song, and He has become my salvation." Regardless of what happened, she believed her faith in God would not be shaken again. She would continue to give thanks to Him, as He alone could insure her salvation. Courtney read for a while, even finding a pen and paper in the nightstand drawer and writing down a couple of verses to memorize. Feeling better than she had in a long time, she turned off the lamp and went to sleep.

The next morning was bright and sunny again, and Courtney felt like God was smiling on them. She fed and changed Grace, then made a second bottle for later using the last of the canister of formula. That meant they only had the small packets left. They had eaten some muffins and fruit they brought with them from the shelter. She prayed they would find more formula that day. She knew that Miah would leave shortly to work in the old building, so she asked if he would mind keeping an eye on the baby, who was sound asleep in the cradle, so she could run over and see if the shelter had gotten formula. Miah told her he didn't need to leave for another thirty minutes, so he headed up to the loft to stay with Grace while Courtney headed over to the shelter.

Going in the back of the building, she was happy to see that there were several empty rooms available. They should have no problem staying at the shelter that night. She headed toward the pantry room. She worried when there were no small diapers available but was thrilled when she found more formula. She picked up the canister and turned around quickly to get back to the baby, then ran right into a man who had come up behind her. She started to apologize, but fear washed over her as she realized who it was. Don!

He snatched her arm, and the formula dropped to the floor and rolled away. He led her out the door of the pantry room. He then took her to one of the empty rooms she had been so happy about only minutes before and closed the door. He stood there looking at her.

"Well, miss," he started with the sarcastic voice he had used with her in the past, "I guess you thought you were done with me, huh? Stupid girl! Where's that little brat you've been trying to pass off as your own?"

Courtney didn't know what to say at first. Then she shook off the fear as her anger took over. "What I do is none of your business! Just leave me alone!"

"Not a chance, sweetheart," Don continued. "You and I have a lot to talk about."

"Well, we can't do it here!" She could hear people talking nearby. "Besides, I have to get back to the baby or someone will call the police."

"Well, what do you suggest, dear?" Don replied.

"There's a bench at the edge of town, near a path into the woods, where no one will bother us," Courtney told him. "Meet me there first thing in the morning. I have to have time to get someone to watch the baby. Come at first light."

Don looked at her suspiciously. "You had better not be lying," he told her meanly. "If I don't find you there, I will go straight to the authorities myself and tell them that you kidnapped the baby you have with you and are not in your right mind. You'll never be rid of me, Courtney . . . Star—whatever you call yourself these days— and you *will* tell me everything you know about me. You shouldn't have been so nosy."

"You killed my mother, didn't you? They found her body, you know." Courtney couldn't stop herself. "Why? She was so good to you."

"I like younger women," Don replied, looking at her with lust. "Besides, I needed the money."

"Money?"

"Insurance money, stupid." Don walked away without another word.

Now Courtney knew his motive. He killed unsuspecting women to get the insurance money and terrorized their teenage daughters!

Courtney believed Don would do exactly as he threatened. She knew she had to make him believe she didn't suspect as much as she did about his past, or get him arrested.

She almost ran out of the shelter, going out the front door. She didn't want him to see her heading to the outreach center. As soon as she was sure Don wasn't following her, she headed back a different way, circling around a couple of times just in case. She calmed herself down, not wanting Miah to know what she had discovered.

When she arrived at the outreach center, she didn't tell him about the altercation with Don, knowing he needed to get to work. She told herself she would tell him later.

"They are supposed to have some formula tomorrow," she told Miah. "So maybe we should stay here tonight and head over there for breakfast." She prayed there would still be formula the next day.

"Sounds good," Miah replied. "I have to get going. I'll stop at Subway and get us a couple of sandwiches on my way back."

After he left, Courtney sat down on the bed, bowed her head, and cried. Was this ever going to be over? She knew she had to meet Don and be done with him once and for all, but how was she going to make it happen?

That night when Miah returned, they ate the sandwiches he brought with him and finished the rest of the fruit they had saved. He had stopped by the shelter for a hot shower, but he looked extremely tired. She tried to remain cheerful, so Miah wouldn't suspect anything. When he told her he was exhausted from all the lifting and carrying, and was ready for bed, she suggested he go up to the loft. She could always tell him about Don in the morning. "I can read better down here," she encouraged him. "And it will be quieter up there."

By the time she had fed and changed the baby, Courtney was getting fretful again. She still didn't have a plan. Grace had fallen asleep, so she put her on the couch that Miah usually slept on, using a blanket to make a little cocoon around her so she couldn't roll off the couch. She sat down on the end of the couch. Finally, she tried to rest, stretching out on the other couch. She still hadn't come up with a plan. She dozed for a bit, knowing she had to leave and get away before Miah woke. And she dreamed.

In her dream, Don was chasing her. She ran and ran until she came to the falls. God stood before her, stopping her and putting his arm around her, telling her to trust in Him. She could hear Don coming, pounding down the path to the falls. But when he got to them, he looked different, brighter somehow, as he ran past them. Before she could make sense of any of it, he ran right over the waterfall! She woke up shaking. Suddenly she knew what she had to do.

She carried the sleeping baby upstairs and placed her in the cradle, then left the bag with her things where she knew Miah would see them. It was already four in the morning, and the light would come quickly once the sun started to rise. She had to get there before Don, had to be waiting. She gave the sleeping baby one last kiss and crept outside, tears flowing down her cheeks.. She headed to the bench at the beginning of the path through the woods, on the outskirts of town. She had no idea how this would all turn out, but she was putting her trust in God.

Chapter 22

It started raining on the way there. At first, street lights lit the way, but the closer Courtney got to the bench near the forest, the darker it got. The wind whipped at her wet clothing, reminding her of another time not so long ago. She was terrified of what was going to happen but trudged on, tears still running down her face. She thought about everyone she cared about: Grace, Miah, Zoey, and the Scotts—everyone.

She was saddened, knowing she had placed a heavy burden on poor Miah if she didn't return. She hadn't even told him her real name, or Grace's circumstances, and he wouldn't know why she left. He might even think that Don had finally found her and taken her away. If she didn't return, he would have to find a home for Grace. All the way to the bench, she prayed . . . that Miah would look harder at faith in God and find strength in it, that he would come to believe in God's Son and eternal salvation, and that he would find a good home for Grace.

Courtney reached the bench where the path led into the forest just before dawn. She tied a plastic shopping bag to the bench. Inside was a piece of white cardboard she had found at the outreach center. In bold letters she had written *Follow the path* with a permanent marker. She headed into the forest.

A short distance from the curve in the path that led to the falls, she spotted an ancient shed back in the woods that she hadn't seen when she and Miah took their walk. It was broken-down and rotting away, but she went inside anyway. A weathered church pew sat along the back wall, protected from the rain by the biggest part of the roof. It was another reminder of the faith she had finally found again . . . another reminder that God was with her. She sat down on it, hoping she still had a little time before Don showed up. She could just see the path winding through the trees from an opening in the opposite wall that had once been a window. The rain had stopped, and all was quiet, except for the chirping of birds. It wouldn't be long, and she prayed silently, asking God to give her strength. And she prayed that she had understood her dream and that God was showing her the only way forward. In the midst of her fear and anxiety, she heard the voice that she had heard the night of the hurricane.

I am here.

The sun was starting to rise when Courtney heard the sound that told her it was time to go. Creeping quietly outside, she stopped and listened. She could hear Don running down the path, so he must have found the note she had left on the bench. He was coming, and despite the dream, she was terrified! As soon as she spotted him, she started jogging in the direction of the waterfall.

She was out of time. She had to put an end to the problems plaguing her, and let God lead her to something better. She was strong in her faith now, knew Jesus as her Savior, and knew her Lord would not forsake her. She remembered the verse she had memorized recently, repeating John 11:25 over and over: *Jesus said to her, "I am the resurrection and the life. He who believes in Me, though he may die, he shall live."*

She had prayed for an answer, and her dream had shown her the way. It had to be the answer she was looking for. Still, it was so risky. She was sorry that it had come to this, but she hoped at the very least Don would stop threatening and harming people. She hoped there was still a chance to stop his madness.

She had felt God's presence, sensed his desire for her to trust in Him. And she had seen Don in a new light, without the ugliness in his heart. It could work for both of them. Besides, even if the worst happened, she would get to meet Jesus and finally see her mom and dad again.

Watching over her shoulder, she knew he was drawing nearer, knew he had seen her. He would not be expecting what she knew awaited them. He would only think she was trying to get away. Even the roar of the falls would not be evident until it was too late. At a full run now, with Don right on her heels, she headed down the short path that she knew ended abruptly.

Suddenly she felt lighter, as if someone was helping her run. She rounded the corner and leapt into thin air! Hearing the startled cry of the man behind her, she knew her plan had worked. Now it was up to Him. Her last thought was, *Thank you, God. Thank you for making me yours. I trust in you!*

She fell through the air, feeling light as a feather. Suddenly the air was filled with a light so bright it brought tears to her eyes. She saw Jesus holding out His arms as if to catch her. She reached out her arms, feeling an incredible sense of peace and joy, but He seemed to be shaking his head no. She opened her mouth to shout His name and thought she heard the words *not yet*.

Suddenly Courtney hit the water with an impact that shook her entire body. Her leap into the air had resulted in her missing the rocks directly below. Still, the current tossed her along like a rag doll. She tried gulping in air when she could and holding her breath every time she went under. Rocks scraped her knees, and twigs caught in her hair, but she was swept along, unable to grab onto anything that would hold against the current.

As she rounded a huge curve in the river, she tried to grab on to a branch hanging out into the water. Gasping for air, she could see a stretch of sand not far away, if she could just fight against the current trying to take her under. *I can do all things through Christ who strengthens me.* The Philippians 4:13 verse fought its way to the surface with her. Holding onto the branch for dear life, she felt it scraping away her skin, pulling out of her fingers. As she was swept into the strong current once more, she hit her head on a large boulder protruding out of the water, and everything went completely black.

Chapter 23

Waiting at the bus station, Miah scanned a local newspaper that someone had left behind. There was a picture on the front page that was vaguely familiar to him. Curious, he looked closer. Yes! It was the beautiful waterfall that he and Star had discovered deep in the woods, just a few days ago. It saddened him to think they would never go there now, and he might never see her again. What had happened to her? Had Don finally found her? He fought the grief that threatened to overwhelm him.

He had waited a couple of days, praying she would return, thinking she would never leave her baby. But, just like his mom, she had left him alone. And on top of that, he had to find a home for this innocent little girl. He was doing his best to care for her, but she deserved a real home, just as he had promised. It was the only thing left he could offer her and Star.

Tossing the paper aside as his bus number was announced, he missed the caption under the picture: *Unknown man is critically injured in fall but lives to tell his story.*

He picked up Grace and made his way to the bus, hoping it would take them to a home for this baby girl.

Tired beyond belief, he climbed the steps to the bus, desperate to get as far away from his memories as he possibly could.

The dog sniffed at the small, wet form on the beach. It was as still as death, but he licked her face and barked.

"Max! Come!" Zoey shouted, running over to Courtney and kneeling down beside her friend. "It's Courtney! Call 911!" she shouted up to her grandparents, who were looking down from the path above. They had separated farther down the river, with Zoey and Max following the river and the Scotts taking the path that wound up and above the waterfall.

Hearing Zoey's shout, the couple quickly dialed 911.

"She's been down here for a couple of days," one of the paramedics informed Zoey. "I don't know how we missed her when we rescued the other fellow who fell. He hit the rocks right at the base of the waterfall when he fell and was pretty broken up. He's telling everyone that it changed his life. Not sure what that's all about." He continued, "This one must have hit the water and traveled along the river. She's pretty battered and scraped, probably from stuff in the water. The current is strong here."

They got her on the stretcher and started the trip back up the river to the ambulance, with Zoey and Max trailing behind.

By the time the Scotts hurried down the path to where they had split from Zoey, the ambulance was already headed to the hospital. They all hurried to where their vehicle was parked and jumped in. Zoey was crying openly.

"They said she took a hard blow to the head and is unconscious," Zoey said through tears. "They think she's been out here for a couple of days, because they found someone else who had fallen over the waterfall. He made it, but he wasn't outside as long as Courtney. They said it has been warmer than usual, but her vitals aren't very good and only time will tell." Zoey rushed to get it all out, trying to calm down, but not succeeding. Then she voiced what they were all wondering. "And where is Grace? Is she gone?" This brought fresh tears.

"We have to get to the hospital, honey," Gramps finally managed. "We just don't have the answers right now." The couple looked at each other anxiously, and Tom could see tears forming in Mary's eyes and running down her cheeks.

"God help her!" she whispered to Tom. And He did.

Epilogue

Courtney looked around her room at the Scotts', remembering how much she had loved it when she arrived six months ago. It was still pretty, but so different. The crib was gone, but she had insisted on keeping the rocking chair in her room and still had days where she sat there and rocked and cried for Grace. For the thousandth time, she wondered where the tiny girl had gone and whether or not she was happy. She knew that Miah would have done everything he could to find her a good home. They had even talked about it. But a piece of her heart would always belong to Grace.

The Scotts swore they would never let Courtney out of their sight again. They had traced the number that Courtney had last called Zoey from, then traveled to Ohio to find her. It was Zoey who insisted they look for the waterfall that Courtney had told her about, thinking her friend might be hiding nearby. It saved her life!

Courtney had finally gotten a copy of her birth certificate, which had been rushed when she was in the hospital and they needed to identify her blood type. Mary and Tom had been instrumental in calling the judge they knew in Florida and rushing it through. Still, she had almost died.

She smiled, because God had become her mainstay. She would never doubt her faith again, never be afraid to turn to God. He was there when the paramedics came, and Courtney had been close to going with Him. The white light had been with her, but the paramedics had pushed it back, and she understood it was not her time yet. God had a different plan for her and had given her a wonderful family to spend the rest of her life with. She would make the most of it and see what He had in store for her. Still, she would never forget the precious little angel she had spent more than a month with, would never stop thinking about her when she saw a rainbow or a bright star twinkling in the night.

As she stood up to go find Zoey, her forever sister, she fingered her locket with the pictures of her and her mom, and her mom and grandmother. Then she felt the newer locket that her grandparents had given her for her birthday, as it rested against the older one. Inside was a picture of Courtney and Grace on one side and Courtney and Zoey on the other. It meant the world to her!

"I love you, Grace," she said out loud as a tear trailed slowly down her cheek. "I always will."

From the Author

I hope you enjoyed *A Leap of Faith*. This story is actually a continuation of one of the characters from a couple of my other novels. In *Amazing Grace*, I focused more on the baby's story and the home that Miah found for her. *Hope Everlasting* continued the story from the view of Miah himself. I wasn't sure about telling Courtney's story, but it kept pestering me until I finally gave in and wrote it down. And who knows—there may be more to come!

God works in mysterious ways, and I never know what direction I'll take when I start a new novel. I'm trying to let God lead the way and use these books to spread *His* Word. I feel so blessed to be able to share this gift that *He* gave me with all of you.

Blessings,

J. C. Lafler

Other Books by
J. C. Lafler:

Lost and Found
A story of faith, love, and survival

The boy's eyes blinked open and slowly focused on the rat. When recognition finally registered, the startled boy sat up, pushed away the bags of garbage and stood up, trembling on shaky legs. Tripping through the garbage, head and heart pounding out painful reminders of life, the boy put as much distance between him and the rat as he could manage.

People don't understand the impact that a simple act of kindness can have on someone. In *Lost and Found*, author J. C. Lafler tells the story of a young boy who finds himself in a big city with no memory of the past and no one to help him. He must find a way to survive, searching for food and water in some of the worst areas of the city. As flashbacks and questions about the past begin to overwhelm him, he leans on the sanctuary of a church and the help of strangers to see him through. *Lost and Found* is one boy's story of finding his way back to faith, hope, and love.

Amazing Grace

Amazing Grace, a story about the life-changing power of faith and forgiveness

He wrapped the old blanket around her, making sure she could still get air, and closed the box carefully to protect her as much as possible from the cold. He placed the box up against the door, looked around to make sure nobody was watching, and walked away. As he went, he prayed silently: Lord, please protect this child and help her to live a happy life. Amen.

In our fast-paced society, it is easy to end up in situations that are beyond our control. Children, especially, are often left to fend for themselves without proper guidance or necessities. In *Amazing Grace*, author J. C. Lafler tells the story of a group of young girls who find themselves in an unloving environment. The oldest girl, eleven-year-old Sarah, takes the lead role in caring for the girls and teaching them about life and faith. A baby left on their doorstep adds additional strain to an already difficult situation, but brings the girls a sense of purpose and togetherness. With the help of her childhood Bible, and fading memories of parents who taught her that faith can get you through most situations, Sarah teaches the girls that belief in God and His resulting grace can overcome almost anything, including an extremely mean and critical guardian. *Amazing Grace* is a story of faith, forgiveness, and discovering love in the most unlikely of places.

Hope Everlasting

Hope Everlasting, a story of faith, HOPE, and love.

In *Hope Everlasting*, by J. C. Lafler, a young runaway struggles with feelings of guilt, abandonment, and worthlessness. Vaguely remembering his mother's belief that "God is with us and there is always hope," he tries to make his way on his own, when a horrible experience as a foster child leaves him no other options. After meeting another runaway and helping the girl with her infant daughter, she disappears, leaving the infant with him. Having no way or means to care for an infant, he leaves her on the doorstep of a home for girls, praying that she will be taken care of. Penniless, with nothing but an old backpack containing all that he owns, he continues his search for a job and a warm place to spend the night. When the last glimmer of hope seems to be disappearing, he wanders onto a farm and finds not only a job, but eventually a loving family and a permanent home. *Hope Everlasting* is a story about the amazing possibilities that exist when we turn to God and believe in His desire to give us a future and hope.

Reader Reviews:

Lost and Found

What an imaginative and beautifully written story. I was totally caught up by the beginning poem and then engrossed as the story unfolded. I loved the way the boy began to feel the love surrounding him . . . slowly, as the petals of a flower opening . . . and then came to the realization that God was actually watching over and loving him via the special "angels" he encountered. The epilogue was such a satisfying surprise! You did a delightful job of sharing God's love for everyone and how He has us in His hands no matter where life leads.

Lost and Found was the first book I read from J.C. Lafler. She expertly pulls you into Alex's dire situation and you feel the emotions of this little boy as though you were walking in his shadow. As I made my way through the book, I kept questioning who the author was because of the brilliant writing. I felt like I was reading a Francine Rivers novel. Few books make me cry and tears welled up many times. It's a quick, heartwarming read. Highly recommend!

Amazing Grace

Amazing Grace is the second novel by J.C. Lafler, and once again she has pulled us into a heart-warming story that will have you quickly turning the pages to find out what will happen next. This author has a way of making you feel the emotions of her characters and it is just what my heart needed. I am looking forward to her next novel.

Amazing Grace is a delightful read. It's a modern day *Little Women* for a school of foster girls. I highly recommend this charming book. It is beautifully written to reveal the simplicity of the cross and God's grace. No matter how life looks or what you've experienced, God's grace is always present and you will believe it by the time you finish this book.

Hope Everlasting

What a pleasure to read J.C. Lafler's books. I loved her first book "Lost and Found" . . . Then I couldn't put down "Amazing Grace." Now we learn the back story of "Amazing Grace" with her most recent "Hope Everlasting." You won't be disappointed while enjoying these books!

I have so enjoyed reading J.C. Lafler's books, Lost and Found, Amazing Grace, and now her latest book,

Hope Everlasting. Her stories are delightful! You won't be disappointed in reading her books!

A lovely story of hope through faith in God . . . I have read all of her books, don't miss this one!

Order Information

REDEMPTION
P R E S S

To order additional copies of this book, please visit
www.redemption-press.com.
Also available on Amazon.com and
BarnesandNoble.com
Or by calling toll-free 1-844-2REDEEM.

9 781683 146612